I'd Kill For You

Copyright

Copyright © 2023 PAIGE LANE
All rights reserved.
ISBN: 9798391630234

Paige Lane

Dedication

To all the people who not only supported me but showed me what could be achieved

This book ends on a cliff hanger which will follow into the second book.

Thank you.

The beginning.

Hallie was in a state, sweat dripping from her forehead, why was this happening. It is as if every time she closed her eyes, she could see the murders taking place. Being able to see how these poor victims are being killed, a voice in the background just shouting words Hallie can't quite make out it's like everything is fuzzy. A scream bellows from Hallie which feels more like a cry for help, dropping to the floor in pain it's as if she is the next victim. "No, no, why are you doing this?" The vision is becoming more and more clear, what the victims looked like before their deaths it's like it's in order, the first victim, the second, so on. Is this an illusion, a nightmare, is Hallie just sleep deprived, or is it another one of the killer's mind games?

As Hallie pulls herself up to the bathroom counter, she looks at herself in the mirror, mascara running down her face from her tears, pale as she has ever looked, she just stares at herself for what feels like a lifetime. "Why?" she asks herself with a tremble in her voice. A voice which feels like is all around her,

"Because Hallie, I have you right where I want you. For you to see everything and the reason behind it."

1

3 months earlier

"BREAKING NEWS. This just in, police have been called to the outskirts of Winchester from a discovery of a body. We are yet to learn what has happened and who the victim is however we are told that the Turtle Bay Park has now been cornered off by police and an investigation has taken place. We are awaiting a response from Winchester constabulary."

"Right, what's happened here?" Hallie Jones was one of the highest detectives in her ranking and one of the hardest workers in the constabulary. Working in the police force since she was 21, Hallie was previously in the Army since she was 16 and began to work her way up in rankings if it wasn't for the death of her team member in Afghanistan. Hallie had incredible features, wavy brown hair with piercing green eyes that when you look in you feel mesmerized by them. Hallie was not one to be messed with though, although her looks can come across cute and approachable, she can turn and make you regret any wrong move you display on her.

"27-year-old female, struck at the head by a hard flat object and stabbed multiple times." Detective Adam Fowler, Hallie's partner in the job, explaining in a monotone not wanting to share his tremble in his throat to what was the most chilling thing about this body. He continues, "Not a robbery as all belongings seems to still be with her, car keys, purse bag even her MacBook. Victims name is Katie Miranda Wilson which is."

"Robert Wilson's daughter?" Hallie interrupted in shock, what would Theodore Wilson's daughter be doing out here?

"That's not the worst part," Fowler added in a slightly more worrying tone, "after Katie was killed, she was placed in a position, like a, I can't really describe it, like a..." before Fowler could explain they were staring down at the victim, well Hallie was, Fowler chose to look away. Katie was sat in an upright position against a tree, all her belongings laid out next to her like someone was examining them however no one had touched anything on the crime scene, the killer had done this. Katie had all clean clothes on and her previous clothes she was wearing were folded up neatly next to her. The killer had got Katie changed, folded her clothes up, laid out all belongings with her laptop screen open like something would play any minute.

"Right, get the victim out of here to be examined and get a confirmed cause of death, all belongings back to the station. I want everything gone through and checked thoroughly. That laptop needs to be sent to IT ASAP, see if the killer has left any traces to why the victim may have been this far away. I need to get a confirmed ID then we need to call Sergeant as he is going to want to know what we are dealing with."

"Does that mean, what I think it means boss?" Fowler asked but the way he asked he already knew what the answer would be.

"It does indeed Fowler, it means that if I am correct, either..."

"The night stalker has an accomplice. Or..." "Or Fowler, we sent the wrong person to prison and the Night Stalker is still out roaming free."

Hallie and Fowler spent that afternoon getting all information on the Night stalker, including all previous killings, every victim, suspect, witness, and location of each event. A large wooden board was wheeled into their office and photos began to hang onto this, maps, information on what had happened. Hallie made it her priority that everything was out so if something was missing, she would know. This case was one that stuck with Hallie for some time, it hit hard when she was investigating it, not only because it was one of the most documented cases in the UK for the century, but it was also because the third killing happened so close to where Hallie had lived, and she knew the victim. 18-year-old George Benson was a troubled lad, no close family, was beaten as a child however seemed to turn out to be one of the most popular kids in his high school. He stood up to what he thought was right and Hallie always believed that there was no reason to his death just he was in the wrong place at the wrong time.

"Right, I need to make a clear look over each case, how we managed to link each one of these deaths to Night stalker." Hallie expressed in a stern tone, she knew that to find him, she needed to not only tread carefully but to get this wrapped up as quick as possible. If Night Stalker killed once, they would kill again.

"Okay, well let's lay out what's happened on this case so we can link it to any similarities from the previous cases?" Fowler asked in a way in which he knew this was the approach they needed to take. Fowler had always admired working with Hallie and enjoyed their partnership. He knew this case would bring up some dark memories they both encountered. Hallie also knew that she would want no other person to work on a case like this than Fowler, the willingness and determination they both had not to mention the intensity between them just shows their chemistry and with a history like theirs you'd be shocked if there wasn't one.

2

Hallie had very little sleep that evening, going nonstop through this case and what had happened to this poor victim. Katie Benson, of all people it could be, why this person. Did the killer, have a connection with Katie, or did they want to hurt someone and get revenge as her father was one of the highest working judges in the country. The Sergeant was briefed on the case and assigned Hallie and Fowler as chief investigators of the case. Awaiting the call from Judge Wilson to confirm the death of his daughter felt like the longest wait we could ask for. The thought of having to go and question the parents was gut wrenching but was a job that had to be done.

"Jones, you're going to want to see this." Fowler seemed in shock, and for whatever reason, his shock was necessary.

Good morning Detective Inspectors, I see you have discovered my latest work, what did you think? I believe it's my best work yet. But I think there is always room for improvement so don't worry you will see me around, well not me I'm sure of that one! I wonder if my nickname you all had for me all those years ago has stuck or whether I will get a new one. I will leave that to you.

"Shit, how have they got my email, how did they get through the security system?" Fowler tried to stay calm but knew this was a step to far.

"Fowler, stop, look at the email who sent it."

"Uh says, 'Sent by Katie M Wilson @10.42pm, 24th February', I, I don't understand. I mean, we have the laptop, we found Katie that morning."

"The killer must have had access to her laptop, either sent it from another computer with her log in or created the email and sent it on a time response so it would send us on a wild goose chase. All I know is that IT have it now and I am getting my hands on that MacBook, I need to find out if it was sent on the laptop or whether it was sent elsewhere. Whoever this killer is, they are smart, and they want to play a game. We just need to find them before anyone else is targeted." As Hallie and Fowler's minds were put to work one question kept appearing. The Night Stalker never approached any person before, just left a trail as to their target. Was there something this killer wanted us to know, is it a different killer? Or could this be just another test. Hallie knew this would blow the media up, and this killer wants the attention.

Hallie is walking so fast she may as well be running and her destination, the IT department. The attempt to find out where this email was sent from was a must and hoping that the killer made a mistake. Just the one slip up so that Hallie can close this case before another innocent victim is taken. Previous cases were all linked in the end and boiled down to a call practically leading the police to the killer.

"Ahh, Detective, was wondering how long it would take for you to come visit. Missed us that much?" Jason Gibb is your typical techy type. Tall, not too big of a build, glasses, blonde fine hair, and blue eyes, not too blue like a cloudy sky blue. Gibb seemed to be more confident since joining the IT department for the police. Left school early, well graduated early shall we say, from the background check he had his teacher thought best to get him out sooner rather than later before he ended up hacking into something he shouldn't have.

"Gibb, no time for the backward forward chit chat I need info about this laptop, can you" before Hallie could finish Gibb interrupted "oh, must be serious, not even a hello". "I'm sorry Gibb but this is important, an anonymous email was sent to Fowler's computer, someone not only had it but sent it whilst the laptop was in this station." "Oh, shit, okay well I understand now, urm well I have only just been given it from forensic so let's have a look." The look on Hallie and Fowler's face shows confusion on both sides. If the laptop was in forensics, then it would be locked up overnight. No one would have access to it till morning. That's one more thing to check, but first if Gibb can show anything.

3

5 years ago

> 'We have some breaking news just in. Police are currently investigating a homicide and have just released the most recent victims' details. Winifred James, a 29-year-old originally from London was studying at the local psychiatric hospital. Family and friends of the victim are distraught that someone would do this to their sweet, kind-hearted girl. Police have released a statement ensuring they are working all hours to catch this person and for anyone who may have any information to contact 101 with the reference Night Stalker or to contact local police station.'

Hallie was distraught. After working tirelessly and thinking they were getting one step closer, another victim is found. That is 7 killings in the space of 7 months. A killing a month. Whoever this person is, they were one step closer to finding. Currently, Hallie and her partner Fowler have 3 suspects and it seems that all have something in common, not a sane sense of mind. As the night draws in Hallie receives a call, she allows the phone to ring for a bit before realising it's someone trying to get a hold of her. Fowler had to interrupt Hallie's deep thought to get her to answer the phone. Its Sergeant Dent, "Can you come to my office, now. You both will want to see and hear this!" What now. Has the Sergeant seen something Hallie and Fowler could've missed. If so, she'd be relieved as it could all be over.

"Sergeant, I am hoping what it is you need us for is good news. Could use some of that?" Hallie said in a tired, worn-out voice. You could see in her eyes that she needed sleep, and that coffee was the only thing keeping her awake. That and these fizz stick drinks which were apparently healthy, but she knew was another way to get caffeine in her system.

"Your idea was good Hallie." Sergeant sounded somewhat proud, which was odd as he was a very old-fashioned man who was stern and would never show any sense of emotion. "My idea sir?" Hallie began to question herself. No amount of sleep could help her remember what ideas she had said let alone if she thought Sergeant was being genuine or sarcastic. "About working with the media and allowing them to share minimal but useful information. It has helped. We have had some people come forward and I need you to listen to this particularly." Towards the end of this sentence the tone went from sounding proud and optimistic to stern. What could this one call have that has made even the Sergeant question himself.

- 101 police information how can I help.
- Urm, hello. I was told to call and give the reference Night Stalker if I had any information.
- Yes, thank you for giving me the reference. What information do you have.
- Well, I don't know whether it is of any use but everyone I have spoken with, well I say everyone I mean Margery and Dawn at lunch told me I must talk with the police. They think I could help.
- I am sure you can help. What is your name for me?
- Oh, where are my manners. My name is Mrs. Pauline Deere, do you need my address or date of birth.
- Not yet Mrs. Deere.
- Oh please, call me Pauline.
- Of course, so tell me Pauline, how do you believe you can help us?
- Well, as I said to Margery and Dawn, I was watching Good Morning Britain on the telly where they said this morning about another killing. Thought just such awful news. Another innocent person taken too soon by, well who knows. Now the telly has only ever said about the killings, never the names or a photo at least. Well, today was different, they showed that

- poor young girls name and then a photo. Now as soon as I heard the name I thought, I know that name. I mean it's not a very common name, but I recognized it and then her photo appeared on the screen, and I instantly recognized her. I immediately wrote down all the other victims' names as a clog was turning in my head. I knew somewhere I knew all these names. Just couldn't think where. Until I found a photo.
- What was the photo of Pauline?
- It was a picture of the psychiatric hospital, and all the names of the people were in it. Where that young girl worked. I knew I'd seen her before.
- Did you visit that hospital Pauline, is that how you know all the victims.
- I did. I saw them weekly, and I feel like there will be more killings now I know. And unsure whether I have done the right thing in calling you today.
- You have done the right thing Pauline. Why do you think you haven't done the right thing?
- Because each of the victim's female and male, my son would tell me their names saying he was in love with each one. And one day how each one broke his heart.
- Your son Pauline? Who is your son.
- He was admitted there as a child. He was troubled and I only wanted what was best for him. I assume he is still there now.
- Pauline, I need you to tell me your son's name.
- His birth name is Harrison Robert Deere. But in the hospital, he was known as Nathan Smith.

"Nathan Smith." The tape was paused by Hallie, she began pacing the room. Mind back in the game. "Nathan Smith, why Nathan Smith?"

"I am assuming for protection purposes." Fowler added. "NO." Hallie stopped in her tracks, no longer was coffee keeping her awake it was adrenaline. "No, what Hallie?" Both Fowler and the Sergeant looked at each other. Sergeant began to interrupt when Hallie stopped him. Writing everything she is saying aloud on the white board, "Nathan Smith, N S. this can't be a coincidence. N S. Night Stalker". Turning back to look at both Fowler and Sergeant's face, they look in disbelief. "Sarg, we need Mrs. Deere to come in now for questioning.

To many connections with this man linking to every victim. Oh, what do we know about this Nathan Smith?" As soon as Hallie said his name something twigged in her brain. It is like she knew who this person was but couldn't figure out where. Maybe she was still overtired or over analysing this. They have a good solid lead, focusing on that might get this case solved.

4

As Gibbs was working through the coding's on the laptop to try and pass the log in to gain access to all information, this seemed to show a struggle for Gibb. This was the part that he could do in seconds but was taking longer for some unknown reason.

"Hallie, I... I am unable to get into this laptop. This coding, I have never seen anything like it before?" Gibbs sounded defeated like this was going to be a challenge.

"Gibb, just do your best, we will get extra security on our computers and just you let us know when you've got access to the victims laptop." Hallie knew that Gibbs was the best in the business and if he was having trouble getting this then this killer knew what they were doing!

"Detectives," a woman's voice, not one Hallie or Fowler recognized. "I'm ever so sorry to interrupt but we have something you need to come see." The young officer looked relatively new to the force, maybe this was her first case. Who knew, but that was the last thing on Hallie's mind right now. "Yes, no worries. Uh, Gibbs just keep me in the loop with any progress you make with this please?"

"Of course Hallie, will make it a priority."

"Thank you, right where are we needed." Hallie asked the young officer in a firm tone. This all seemed like de-ja-vu, maybe that's how the killer wanted this to be.

As Hallie and Fowler were following the young officer it felt like something had twigged in Hallie's brain. Something wasn't adding up. The email, the fact the killer left all possession. It is as if this is just a big game, and there was going to be a new turn.

As they enter the back room of the interrogation room, they are looking at the screens. "That is," but before Fowler could finish, "Judge Theodore Wilson, and his wife yes." Hallie could see how distraught both the parents were. She knew Judge Wilson well. He was the judge for her first ever trial she had to testify in as a police officer for a killing. His big, stocky build made him look at a first glance a man you do not want to be on the wrong side of. Judge Wilson helped Hallie in more ways she can describe. So, seeing him look defeated, upset and just so down was very hard on Hallie.

"Do you need a minute?" Fowler asked in a caring, compassionate tone. He also knew what Judge Wilson meant to Hallie.

"No, no, I'm okay, thanks" looking up at Fowler they lock eyes, all she wanted right now was someone. But she knew she had to stay professional. Sat also in the room was the Sergeant, Simon who dealt with the tapes for any interrogations being held, Fowler and Hallie.

"Sarg, can I..." Before Hallie could finish his answer was immediate.

"I would talk to them both myself, but you are in charge of this case, thought best coming from you both." His look at Hallie and Fowler gave a sense of trust and reassurance.

"Are you sure you want to talk to them. I don't mind, I know the relationship, I just don't want to see you upset." Fowler pulled Hallie aside to the wall and asked as they left the back room to head into the interrogation room.

"What more reason why it shouldn't come from me. Let's just get this bit over and done with, for all we know they might have some insight to why Katie was there." Hallie had faced some challenges in her life but talking with the victim's parents was always a hard pill to swallow. The upset, guilt, the 'why haven't you done more to find who has done this' well, she just knew this judge was a tough cookie to crack, the loss of his only child must be hitting hard.

"Judge Wilson, Mrs. Wilson, I would firstly like to share my condolences and sorry for your loss of Katie, we can only imagine what you are both going through." Hallie knew she needed to keep a professional manner as she knew Judge Wilson well.

"Thank you, Hal- well detective should we say." Judge Wilson refrained from using a first name basis.

"I know this must be beyond difficult for you both but any information you may have of Katie could help us massively to find out who could've done this to her." Fowler began, he was good at interrogation, not that this was one, but he had a knack to get the truth from people. "Do you have any idea as to why Katie was at that park, so far from her campus and even home?"

"Katie would always tell us where she was going or what she was up to for the day, we were very close," her mother added holding back the tears. "She explained she had a project that afternoon, as she studied psychology at the university, and she was getting ready for her placements. Katie would tell us that her project was on mental health and disabilities. Katie would need to learn what goes on in their minds to cause them to do, well I have no idea what they do but Katie was going into the line of work to help people, talk about their problems."

Fowler introjected, "Mrs. Wilson, do you know if Katie was meeting someone for this project or where she was beginning her placement?"

"Yes, she mentioned she had a meeting with a nurse who worked at St Catherine's, a mental institution. Katie and this nurse, well we have met the nurse before haven't we Rob?" Mrs. Wilson looks up to her husband, usually it was Judge Wilson who was the talker, but since this meeting, not a word has left his mouth about Katie.

"Uh, yes sorry, mind was wondering. The nurse was Parker Fields. Graduated about 7 years ago and became a nurse/ mental health adviser at the hospital. I shared concerns at first about Katie going there, I knew this was the line of work she wanted to do, you know make a difference and all that, she thought she could help people, give them a new lease of life, Katie is a caring sole and always has been. Sorry, was." The mood changed instantly, Judge Wilson and his wife were so proud of their daughter and hearing them talk about her in present tense just shows that they were grieving, they lost the one thing they loved the most.

"Thank you, to both of you for coming in, I know timing isn't the best but if we need anything else we will call, and if there is anything we can do for you both please, just let us know." Hallie looking square in the eyes of both Judge and Mrs. Wilson.

"Thank you detective, we wouldn't want anyone else on this case. Just promise us one thing, you'll find that son of a bitch who killed our only child."

5

"Well, that went better than I thought." Hallie said, it was a lie of course but she thought she could ease the tension.

"Yeah, you could say that, so you thinking what I'm thinking?" Fowler added, he liked that him and Hallie thought alike.

"Time to meet this Nurse I think."

"I'll drive" Fowler added, maybe him driving wasn't such a bad idea as Hallie's mind was all over the show. For some reason something was niggling her brain, like something needed to come out but she just couldn't pinpoint what it was. It's like she is just walking through a deep, misty fog. There is damp in the air, she hears a scream. Looking around, nothing, nobody in sight. Another scream. "Hello?" Hallie questioned herself, the scream was someone in pain, struggling. "Help me!" a soft but worried voice appeared. Like an echo in the shadows. "Where are you?" Hallie began to run into the fog.

"Hallie, you alright?" Fowler had his hand firmly on Hallie's leg, not too tight of a grip but like a nice force.

"Yeah, my mind just wondered that's all." Hallie had a tremble in her tone, she had never had any daydream like that before, that felt too real.

"You make me worry about you; you know that." Fowler's hand still not moved from Hallie's leg. The sense of security Hallie felt just from Fowler's touch was unreal, she didn't want to move just in case he moved his hand back. Hallie tried not to read too much into it.

"Yeah, worry about myself sometimes too." Looking over at Fowler's side profile taking in his looks Hallie had never looked at him this way. She smirked as Fowler briefly looked at her whilst still driving.

"What, have I got something on my face? Knew I shouldn't have had that Doughnut, bet its sugar." He was right, there was a small amount of sugar on his left cheek. Hallie gently brushed her hand over his cheek to wipe it off. The car had stopped and was silent. Both just looking, then Hallie's phone began to ring making them both jump.

"Shit, that's loud!" Hallie said annoyingly. For once she was enjoying a moment alone.

"Yep," Hallie's tone was angry, and Fowler just laughed.

"Detective, where are you?" It was Sergeant, now she began to talk a bit more politely. "Sorry sir, I did try to call, Fowler and I have just got to St Catherine's to speak with this nurse the victim's parents spoke about. From what they were saying that would've been the last person she would've seen."

"Right, well I need you both back here asap when done there, media is kicking our asses for not disclosing everything. Just hope you find something there."

"Yes sir, will keep you posted." Hallie hung up the phone and turned back to Fowler who already knew that he missed his chance in the moment.

"Right, let's go find this Parker bloke."

6

As Hallie and Fowler approached the doors to St Cathrine's Hospital, it was like something out of a movie. The doors were white with glass panels in, and as you entered the building a white reception room with photos of landscapes and mountains scattered around the room. "Why does it feel like I have been here before?" Hallie questioned herself. She felt like she knew this place but would've remembered it if she'd been here.

"Maybe an old case, we have seen some variety of people remember," As Fowler was about to continue his sentence, he was rudely interrupted.

"We don't like to describe people in that manner, especially if you are visiting this building. Least you could do is show some respect, God." A woman appeared behind the reception desk with a high attitude. She was a petite woman, red hair, and a small amount of freckles cluster around her nose.

"Oh ma'am, I wasn't talking about..."

"I know exactly what you were insinuating, and I will not have it, not here nor anywhere if around me!" Fowler looked over to Hallie, all Hallie could do was show a smirk at him.

"Hello, miss?" Hallie asked, she knew if Fowler kept talking she would dig himself a deeper hole.

"Kirk, Mrs. Kirk, and who are you here visiting, not that YOUR negativity will help them" Looking directly at Fowler.

"Okay, well how about we start again then Mrs. Kirk, my name is Detective Inspector Jones, and this is my partner Detective Inspector

Fowler, and we are not here to see any patients, a staff member to be exact, now how about we cut the attitude you are giving us and point us in the direction of a Parker Fields." Hallie kept a calm tone, but you knew that she was a force to be reckoned with.

"Uh, yes my apologies Detectives, I just?"

"You listened into a conversation that had nothing to do with this hospital and assumed we was bad mouthing patients." Hallie could've continued but time was of the essence. "Now, Mrs. Kirk, what direction are we heading in?"

"Yes of course, straight down the hall, take the elevator and head to the 5th floor. I will call the desk now to have Dr Parker meet you there."

"Thank you" Hallie began to walk away with Fowler when they got in the elevator. "Dug yourself a hole there didn't ya!"

"Fuck off Hal, no matter what I said she'd got the wrong end of it."

"Ooo, someone is touchy today. Have you not had your beauty sleep?" Hallie joked, but as she looked up at Fowler no smile appeared on his face.

"Hey, I was joking, what's going on?"

"Nothing, sorry, lot on my mind especially this case, the killer playing fucking mind games again, just," the elevator doors opened, and silence was clear, you could hear a pin drop. "How about we have a drink later, we both have history with this case, and I know for a fact you're not yourself either?" As Fowler looked down at Hallie, she couldn't make eye contact.

"Okay, but I am not going to the pub!"

"Fine, my place after work, believe me I got enough alcohol to fill a brewery." Fowler smirks,

"Your place it is, wait. There he is." Parker Fields was dealing with a patient when he caught Hallie's eye.

"Ah, detectives, Ms. Kirk told me you were on your way up. Going to apologies now for her, divorce hitting her hard. Please, this way." Parker showed his way down the long corridor whilst talking, the walls were still white but at least this floor had photos of real people and their smiles, well some smiles.

"We believe you're a nurse here,"

"Doctor, graduated last year."

"My apologies, doctor, we were told you knew a Miss Katie Wilson, may we ask you a few questions about your relationship?" Parker froze, the smile he had was now gone, his tanned skin now looked like he had just come down with an illness.

"Please tell me, it wasn't Katie who... Who was found the other night?" Parker had a tremor in his voice, he sounded more worried than anything.

"Is there somewhere we can talk, maybe a bit more private?" Fowler asked Parker knowing he mustn't have heard the news just yet.

"Yes, my office, come this way." Parkers, office was a warm sage green with photos of animals around it and a photo on his desk of a woman sat on a mountain with a view. All you could see was the back of her head which was long blonde hair, very similar to Katie's.

"I am sorry to tell you Doctor Fields,"

"Parker, please, call me Parker." Parker insisted,

"Sorry, Parker, yes it was Katie who was found dead at the park last week. We are so sorry, but we must ask you some questions if that is okay." Hallie knew by just looking at him how upset he was, but she needed answers and needed them fast.

"Ye-Yes, I knew Katie very well. She had worked with me on her training in mental health, I told her I worked here and dealt with patients all day every day and this would be a good place for her to learn and grow. We had a close relationship, we even went on holiday together about 4 months ago,"

"Is that her in the photo here?" Fowler asked already knowing the answer, least she looked more alive in the photo than how he had seen her.

"Yes, wait before you think anything more, we were just friends, she was seeing someone and this was a work holiday, we went with a few other colleagues. Plus, that was a gift from Katie, look at the back." Fowler picked up the photo frame, read the back then passed it to Hallie.

'Dear P, thank you again for all you do, I will be forever grateful, love Katie'.

"You must have meant a lot to her?" Hallie asked looking over at Parker trying to read his emotions.

"Think we meant a lot to each other, I knew how hard it was to get

I'd Kill For You

into a place like this, but she had a talent, and she had the love of making a difference in helping people, you don't see that every day."

"You mentioned earlier that Katie was seeing someone, did she ever mention who this someone was?"

"His name was Alex something, uh shit, she has told me his last name before, wait" Parker went over to the filling cabinet, pulled out a grey file and scanned through it. "Alex Jonoski, he is down as one of her emergency contacts, would you like this? This has every bit of info on Katie that she needed us to know, might help?"

"That would be great Parker, thank you. We see you are a busy man so we will leave you to it, just one more thing would like to ask before we go, do you know anyone that could be out to want to hurt Katie or harm her or her family in any way?"

"No, I don't, I mean she was so lovely to everyone and everything, I have never met a more caring person, even the patients loved her, my goodness Carter!"

"I'm sorry?" Hallie asked, looking over at Fowler then back to Parker.

"I'm sorry, Carter is a patent here who worked with Katie, he really took a shine to her. How am I going to tell him?"

"I wouldn't just yet, wait until we have some more info or even her killer, then at least he will know the whole information."

"Yes, good idea."

"We will see you again Parker, take care." Hallie walked back to the elevator with the grey folder. Both walking back to the car, no one on the front desk, kind of a good thing otherwise Fowler might as well dig back up that hole he dug himself and hop into it.

"Any of that feel normal to you?" Fowler asked knowing something was off.

"Nothing is normal about our job, but no, that wasn't normal." Hallie scanning through the grey folder, "let's take this back to the station, see if they can get any info off it." It was already 9pm and neither Hallie nor Fowler had eaten. As they dropped the file back to the station, no more info from IT about that laptop, nothing more they can do tonight.

"Fancy a Chinese and a drink, I'm bloody starving."

"You read my mind; I'll order it now." Fowler rung through the

Chinese and put their order through. He knew her order off by heart the number of late nights they worked together.

7

Fowler lived in a beautiful house in the country, very secluded and isolated but perfect if you want to be alone and just enjoy nature. The house was handed down to him by his father who was beyond proud when he became a police officer after the army, he bought him a house where he was being stationed as a congratulations. Fowler had a loving family who all cared for each other and took time to see each other. This was the opposite for Hallie. Hallie was an orphan, she had no one, she can't remember most of her childhood as most of it is blanked out, she was told by a therapist this was most probably trauma that's she has tried to close off and forget, which successfully she did.

As Hallie walked into Fowler's house she knew where she was going, straight for the kitchen to dish up her food and Fowler got her a beer. They had done this often when working late. Neither had partners or someone to go home to, not even a pet.

"What a day." Hallie sighed, all she wanted to do was curl up in a ball and sleep, but her insomnia caused her to never really sleep well.

"You're telling me, this case is weird, the people are weird, I just, it feels different but so similar to last time." Fowler looked up at Hallie and she was in a daze. "Hal, you alright?"

"Huh, yeah, sorry was just thinking, why would that Parker give us all of Katie's info, and why wouldn't he mention he saw her that day but on the Rota, he was the only one working not Katie she was signed as off?" Hallie's cogs were turning she knew something wasn't adding up.

Round 2 of drinks- whiskey

"And why would Parker have a photo of Katie on his desk, when he knows she is with someone, and they are just 'friends'?" Fowler implied. "I mean they could just be friends but definitely something more going on there, surely?" Hallie downed her whiskey and poured herself and Fowler another.

Round 6 of drinks-

Work was out the equation now, the topic of conversation was each other. "Okay, okay, you answer me this then Hal, why is it that anyone and I mean anyone that tries to get close to you, you shut down so fast?"

"What's it to you Adam?"

"Well, I know you, and well let's just say you are not a sight for sore eyes, I just can't get over how no one has nabbed you up yet?" The speech slightly slurred but still valid point.

"I just, don't really, I'm not the relationship type, I struggle to trust, been alone for my life so figured that's the way it's meant to be." Hallie stumbled, the drinks were numbing her pain and she knew it. Fowler noticed too.

"Hey, look at me, you are so amazing, caring, loving, and fucking beautiful. You deserve someone who is going to give what you give to everyone back. You need a," as Fowler was talking, he was closer to Hallie, he could smell her coconut shampoo, looking into her eyes, Hallie's eyes fixed on Fowler's she could see the tinge of green in his eyes. "You Hal, are just perfect." Fowler's tone went quiet, like a whisper.

"No body is perfect,"

"You are to me." Fowler had used his hand to gently brush a few strands of Hallie's hair out of her face and tuck behind her ear. He pulled her closer and his hand under her chin guiding her lips to his. Their kiss was subtle, and short. Was a gentle couple of kisses. As they both slowly moved away from each other they locked eyes again and moved back in with speed, this kiss was passionate. Fowler had grabbed Hallie under her arms and lifted her. Hallie's legs wrapped around his waist she could feel his muscle between her thighs. She could also feel something else hard against her. Fowler carried her to the bedroom whilst still kissing her and laid her on the bed. Hallie knew what she wanted, and Adam Fowler was the only thing she wanted right now. They both undressed and Fowler was kissing Hallie, moving down her neck, to her breasts, down her stomach, "fuck" Hallie moaned, he knew what he was doing, and my god he was doing it so well. Both were under the sheets of Fowler's bed, sweaty but the tension they both had for each other it was surprising this didn't happen sooner.

Fowler had Hallie, after all this time, after numerous attempts to tell her how he felt, what better way than to show her. Hallie knew this shouldn't be happening, she could've stopped it but couldn't at the same time, this was just too good to stop. As both were passionately having sex Fowler was dominating, for once he was the one in command. Hallie had always been his superior and now he was able to have Hallie. "You don't know how long I've waited for this!" Fowler breathed into Hallie's ear. Their bodies close, sweat dripped from both and Hallie begged him, she wanted more as did he.

"That was..."

"It was indeed," Fowler added as both lay on the bed naked and out of breath. They knew it shouldn't have happened, they were partners, but neither could deny how good that was! "It's late, you should just stay here tonight?" Fowler questioned but knew that he could easily make her stay.

"Can I just borrow something to sleep in?" Hallie looked over at Fowler to see a big smirk on his face, she knew all he was thinking was for her to just stay naked, the longer he had in this moment the better and for Hallie, she felt all her troubles had gone and she was safe here.

"Okay, well I'm going to take a shower then can call it a night?" Fowler stood up and walked to his en-suite walk in shower, as he walked in Hallie couldn't help but eye up this tall naked figure and this wasn't a sight for sore eyes. Fowler left the door slightly cracked open, Hallie knew this was an obvious move for her to get up and peak, but she took it one step further. The solid wooden door slid wide open, Fowler facing the back wall looking up at the waterfall shower head. Hallie strolled across the shower and joined Fowler, kissing his back as she wasn't tall enough to reach his head. Fowler turned to face

Hallie,

"Didn't get enough in the bed then?"

"Oh, I did, but I'm not missing out on any more opportunities like this, besides, you look good wet." Hallie had a devilish look to her but knew she enjoyed someone else taking control.

8

The next morning Hallie woke from the best sleep she had could ever remember. Hallie had severe sleep insomnia which caused her to have horrible nightmares. As she looked up, her head was still on Fowler's bare chest. They had not only slept together but had one busy night. Hallie felt content, safe, like she really didn't want to move. Looked down at her watch showing 6:30am, that's a lay in for her! As she began to move to get up Fowler's arms hugged her even tighter.

"I'll make us some coffee; we need to get into work." Hallie whispered; Fowler began to wake up.

"I'll make the coffee, you stay here in bed, think that's the first time I have had a full night sleep in this bed!"

"Yeah, think that's the first time I've ever had a full night sleep."

"Well, we can't really say was a full night of sleeping now was it!" Fowler looked to Hallie with a smirk, he knew how much he cared about that woman, and she was finally able to start opening up more. "Well, definitely a night to remember" Fowler kissed Hallie on the forehead before heading to the kitchen, coffee would be needed for today regardless.

"Hopefully not the last?" she questioned, she needed to know his views before she could open up even a little bit.

"Definitely not the last, I'd have you move in today if I could." Fowler meant what he said, but knew he wasn't in a rush with Hallie. He came back and kissed Hallie gently on her lips, headed downstairs to make them both a coffee Hallie laid there staring at the ceiling, and began to get dressed in yesterday's clothes. Luckily, she still looked presentable, sipping her coffee reading over the victim's case file. However, something caught Hallie's eye, something that she hadn't noticed before. "Adam, come take a look at this?"

"What you found?" Fowler came behind her arms either side of her head placed on hers. Hallie felt his warmth and tried to stay focused.

"This, I read through it but must've missed this." Hallie pointed at the document which read '...in conclusion to this, my main ambition is to graduate and get my medical license, but the real reason is to find my brother and his reason for trying to kill me all those years ago.' "I'm sorry, her what!" Fowler got his head closer to the paper to re-read that sentence.

"The Wilson's always said in everyday life, Katie was their only child, their miracle child? Why would they not say they had another child?" There were so many questions even Hallie didn't have the answers to. Hallie's eye line went straight for Fowler's, "we need to get to the station, now!"

The drive to the station wasn't very long but the whole journey Fowler had his hand on Hallie's leg. "Okay, well one thing we need to talk about, is this." Looking down at her leg then back up to Fowler's eye line,

"You best not be saying what I think your gunna say Hal, because I swear to god, I haven't waited all these years for you to..."

"Will you just breathe, all I was going to say, we need to keep this under wraps, just until we solve this case, then we can see where it is going from there." Hallie kept eye contact on Fowler, but he was trying to keep an eye on the road. You could see the smile he had even if he wasn't trying to show it.

"You just need to remember, I am still your boss,"

"Not in my bed you're not, think I made myself very clear of that." Hallie couldn't help her smile, she had butterflies all around her, she knew she wanted him back in bed but soon as she began to imagine it, they were at the station.

"Where have you been?" Sergeant shouted from his office, didn't move from his desk but expected Hallie and Fowler to go straight in. "You both best not have pulled an all-nighter again, I need you alert for this case. I don't give a shit if you think it helps, it doesn't and,"

"Sir, just going to stop you there, we have something you're going to want to hear." Hallie knew the time to shut him up, Sergeant was known to rant on and on. "The Wilson's lied, not only to us but to every press conference and everyone they probably knew." Hallie was pissed off and Sergeant could see this. He knew she had nothing but high praises for Judge Wilson, "go on," he added. "Well sir, we found this" Hallie put this on Sergeant desk for him to read.

"Fuck."

That was all that left his mouth, no explanation, no are you sure, just the word Fuck.

"Sir, did you already know this?" Hallie asked with a look confusion on her face.

"There were rumours years ago, back when the Wilson's moved here but never confirmed." The Sergeant held his hand to his forehead and began to pace. "There was a suicide case back I'd say around 18 years ago, big case it was at the time. Poor bloke was sent crazy, convicted of something he didn't do. Anyways, he was having a rough time and a doctor had prescribed some pills to help him sleep. The doctor who was corrupt anyway thought he was a hero and thought he'd be better dead. So, he gave him something else knowing he had a heart condition to just stop his heart. Made it look like suicide, an overdose. Was Judge Wilson's first case over here and he got that man sent down for life for that. People questioned him but the evidence was there, and he knew it. At his first social gathering he and his wife explained they would move here with their daughter. But their daughter kept mentioning someone called James. Her parents said was her imaginary friend. That is where the rumour started."

"So, you are saying that people thought they had another child, but they said they didn't?" Fowler questioned.

"Exactly, so that means, they lied."

"They did indeed sir, and we need to see the Wilson's immediately." Hallie didn't question this, she knew what needed to be done, and no matter her relationship with the Wilson's, she was determined to get the truth.

Three sharp knocks on Sergeant's door startled both Hallie and Fowler, "I'm so sorry detectives, sir, but you need to come now and see this." The same young detective that found Hallie and Fowler before, but she looks concerned now.

Both Hallie and the Sergeant were following the young detective to the IT department. Hallie was hoping Gibb had cracked the laptop and got us a lead to who this is.

"Gibb, what you found." Fowler asked Hallie right behind him.

"Detectives, Sir, I spent the evening trying to crack this coding. It was a challenge to say the least I'll give you that. Soon as I got through this morning this was on the screen, I wasn't going to carry on without your say."

Confusion lay across all three of their faces. Gibb span the laptop screen around. A big present which was blue wrapping paper, pink vertical stripes and a big red bow sit on the top with a message below,

'Congratulations on cracking the code, here is your prize. Click it.'

Hallie was the one to step forward to the laptop and as she was just about to click the prize, "What are you doing?" Fowler asked stopping Hallie,

"What does it look like, I'm finding out what this is?"

"Hallie, think, this killer is a master at mind games, what if this is destructs or you click it and something else... Let me"

"Yeah, nice try" Hallie reached straight for the laptop and clicked the prize.

"Well?" the sergeant asked, curiosity taking over, and he began to step forward to look over Hallie's shoulder.

"They are... coordinators sir, someone get me a map." The young detective ran to Hallie's aid with a map. "Thank you, miss?"

"Gardener mam." The young detective had a relatively high-pitched voice, but she was young and looked familiar to Hallie, but there was no time to think into that now.

"28, 36, 8, 66 and 92. South Grange Park Farm. Why there?" Hallie questioned and marked a pinpoint on Turtle Bay Park.

"Detective's!" Gibb's voice raised to get the attention. "Look."

Another message appeared on the laptop.

'Come find me and hope you're not too late detectives.'

An image appeared on the screen of Katie and a man with rich dark brown hair, blue eyes judging by the photo this was Alex Jonoski, Katie's boyfriend.

"I will call it in." The Sergeant added walking fast on the phone.

"Let's go, get your keys." Hallie indicated to Fowler, and they left the room running to the car.

9

This was a high-speed pursuit to South Grange Park Farm; time was of the essence as Hallie had Gibb on her phone. "Gibb, anything else."

"Unfortunately not detective. I am in the computer, it looked like a virus, or something just implanted on the laptop for certain amount of time. I can't find any trace of this, of the old coding or anything. It is like it has vanished. Leave it with me, anything I find will send straight over to you."

"Thank you Gibb." As Hallie hung up the call another came through. "Yeah," Hallie put the call straight on speaker.

"Detective, two officers have arrived at South Grange, they have found Alex."

"In what condition is he in?"

"Left for dead. Paramedics have just reached him, weak pulse currently attempting CPR. What is your ETA?"

"2 minutes Sir,"

"Well, this man hasn't got two minutes. Keep me posted"

"Yes sir." Hallie looked at Fowler then back at her phone. "Never before did Night Stalker leave someone alive or nearly dead. This fucked up killer is playing a new game."

"We're here." Fowler and Hallie jumped out of the black Mercedes and went straight to the scene. The look from the paramedics and the officers who were on the scene first both Hallie and Fowler knew he was dead.

"Get forensics out here this place cornered off."

"Yes ma'am." Fowler knew the drill. Their night last night felt like a lifetime ago, like it hadn't happened. This case was going to take its toll on them both.

"Fowler, come take a look at this?" Hallie was close to the body. Once again, all his belongings, phone, wallet, keys but something odd also. A tiny bottle lay next to the victim's body. Hallie reached for her back pocket, photographed the bottle before putting on a blue surgical glove and picking it up. The bottle displayed writing when Hallie turned the tag over.

'Drink me'

Hallie stood up and looked closely at the bottle. "That's like that kid's movie... What's it called?" "Alice in Wonderland. My question is, why?" Hallie began to look around the body to see if any clues were hidden maybe something the killer left. Anything.

"Detectives!" One of the forensic team called both Hallie and Fowler over to the van. "Jameson, nice to see you back doing what you do best." Fowler knew Jameson well, they went to high school together and had the odd few cases together, mainly the high-profile ones.

"It is indeed. Shame it is always in these circumstances. Hallie, looking beautiful as ever."

A slight blush appeared over Hallie's face "Same for yourself Jameson. What you got?"

"Straight to the point as per usual. Fiery one your partner Fowler. Well, second killing but this one was left for dead pretty much. Will have to get the body back to the lab but poisoned. With what though, even my tests show inconclusive. I have run this in the lab, nothing to give me a definite answer. He has been a tied up for some time, bruises around the hands and feet."

"Okay, soon as he is back and you have done your work, let us know when you have more info. Thank you, Jameson." Hallie began to walk off, she needed time to think, get all her information as to why the killer was playing such a game and why these people?

"She is something isn't she." Jameson's comment shook Fowler as looked over at Jameson with jealousy but then back at Hallie knowing she was his.

"We need to go back to the station. Get all evidence together from both victims and from the old case. Need everything laid out in front of us, enough of this shit, he's playing a fucking game, and we are going to beat it." Hallie had enough and Fowler wasn't about to question her.

"I'll get the car."

Hallie's phone began to ring, making her jump due to her being in such deep thought. "What you got?" "I ran a tox screen on Katie's body whilst completing the postmortem and she had a high case of Isocyanic acid in her system. It's an odd one as she's a nonsmoker so would usually see that in smokers. The amount ingested into her body either she was injected or drunk in a formula." "Drunk it?" As those words left Hallie's she looked for Fowler knowing this person was using the same drug as the other victim. "Okay, thank you. Another victim is on the way to you as we speak, I have attached a piece of evidence. Can you test this for the same as to what you found in Katie's system?" "Yes Ma'am."

10

Back in the station both Hallie and Fowler had all the evidence laid out. Each victim had their own board with all information, from family, friends to the place of death. Looking over at Katie Wilson's board had a blank photo with the name James below and a question mark. Knowing she was in contact with someone who was potentially her brother could be a big lead. He could have more information or even be the killer. There were too many what ifs and not enough certainty. They had been going through all the evidence for around four hours now. Awaiting the call from the officers who are watching the Wilson household for both Judge Wilson and his wife to be home so both Hallie and Fowler can get some answers from them.

"We need to find out who this is?" pointing at the blank photo labelled James on Katie Wilson's board, "He must go under another's name, otherwise her parents would suspect something." Hallie was pacing the room talking her thoughts aloud. "Let me see her contact list of who she may have been messaging, could be just text or social media." Fowler handed over Katie's phone which had not long been released from IT. As Hallie scanned all socials, messages, and call log one thing popped up and that was a contact with just a question mark for its name. Pulling out her phone to call for Gibb to bring his laptop up to get an IP address for this contact Fowler attempts to interrupt.

"Gibb, how long would it take you to get all information on this contact?"

"I would say hour or two to sync up and get every detail I know." Gibb was very good at his job, everyone knew it, but this case was a tough one for him already and Hallie was sure there would be more curve balls thrown their way.

"Detective Jones, just to make you aware both Judge Wilson and Mrs. Wilson are home for the night."

"Thank you, we will be there shortly. Grab your keys, we are off to get some truths from a family of lies."

"Let's go." Fowler enjoyed their pursuits, any time alone together he enjoyed really but last night felt like a lifetime ago for him. He knew this case was important and timing wasn't the best but couldn't deny his growth of feelings towards Hallie.

Three knocks on the big solid oak wooden door waiting for an invitation inside. Both gestured into the lounge area where both Wilson's sat, the maid had let both Hallie and Fowler in. "Detectives, please come in. Would you care for a drink?" Mrs. Wilson was always a caring person and had everyone's best interest at heart.

"No thank you Mrs. Wilson, still on the clock here. This will only be a short visit just in need of some additional information if that's okay with yourselves?" Hallie knew how to word in a way she come across kind yet could switch any moment to the unexpected.

"Yes of course, anything to help we can?" Mrs. Wilson insisted, yet still Judge Wilson remained quiet.

"Firstly, I am sure you both heard of the second killing from today. Another victim found in a similar way to your daughter." Hallie awaited a reaction before continuing, both her and Fowler were good at reading facial expressions and both Wilson's remained quiet, Hallie's que to continue. "What can you tell me about Katie's boyfriend?"

"Alex," Judge Wilson piped up looking in disbelief "It wasn't that boy found, was it?"

"I am afraid it is sir, what can you tell us about him. How his and Katie's relationship had been, any bickering, fighting, any enemies you know of?"

"No, not that we know of. They were a lovely couple; we had no problems with him did we Rob?"

"No, none. They had bickered occasionally but had been good for months."

"Their bickering, was it ever over something big or just a lovers quarrel?" Fowler now asked questions, this was a good time for him to interject so Hallie could read the Wilson's reactions.

"The last big argument they had was over that holiday to the mountains Katie had with work. Alex was jealous he couldn't go and got bit protective of her. But Parker assured him she would be okay, and it was for work, a reward for her hard work also. I think that helped him."

"So, Parker and Alex knew each other?"

"Yes, Alex was the one who introduced them together. He knew of Parker through school I believe, Alex was just friends with Katie at the time, she mentioned to him on a date the line of work she wanted to do and arranged for them all to meet. Lovely boy that Parker."

"I see, is there anything else you could tell us about Alex, anything you may have noticed is a bit usual?"

"Well, I remember before Katie went out for work the day, she, she…" Mrs. Wilson couldn't say the word dead or missing. Still in disbelief of her daughter being dead. Grief is a hard thing. "Anyway, she had mentioned she was meeting Alex that evening and how she hadn't heard from him in a couple days, she thought because of his job. He is a marine biologist and travelled a lot."

"Thank you, and just one more question. What can you tell me about your son James?"

11

10 years ago

"Right, you lot listen in. You have all been briefed on the mission and the target. The aim is to get in and out as quickly and swiftly as possible. Target is said to be based in the centre of the building. His men working around him will be heavily armed. This mission has been a bitch but has been an honour serving with you all. Once target is extracted, head back to base and we fly home."

An uproar of cheer from this message from Lance Corporal Harris. Harris knew it was time to take his team home. They had suffered far too many losses from this mission, so it was time to get it done and go home.

"Nice speech sir."

"Thank you, Fowler, you ready for this."

"If it means going home then think we are beyond ready."

Fowler was also a Lance Corporal however Harris ranked slightly higher than him which Fowler was more than happy with.

"Get your gear ready, we arrive in 2 minutes" Harris shouted over the rough terrain of the stubble stone road. The lorry was throwing everyone around but being out in Afghanistan for this long they were used to it.

"Right, you lot let's move. We meet up with Captain Granger and his team on the east side, keep your eye out and gun loaded. They will put up a fight."

The building they were entering looked derelict but both Fowler and Harris had it memorized. From where each door was, the floor plan to even the easiest escape route if needed on each floor. The mission was to extract victims being held hostage by Fladir Kirbanion. Fladir was a terrorist leader of a gang attempting to take over this side of the country. Killing many innocent victims who refuse to join and fight. Fladir had 2 hostages who he had hijacked on a rescue mission, Doctor Ashira Hague, and Lance Corporal Hallie Jones.

"Extract the hostages without causing any commotion. We have Captain Granger's team working with us surrounding the building. Let's get these out." Fowler whispered through his mic which led to his 6 other team members on special force earpieces. Hallie was a part of special forces team but insisted she go with the doctor to the hospital before it was hijacked by Fladir's men.

Slowly and quietly, special forces are making their way through the building. They knew where Hallie and Doctor Hague were, they just had to get there without being targeted. Killing every person who got in there way as silently as they could they were in the heart of the building. Harris signals a halt as he peers around the corner, then a follow me gesture with his hand to make the team aware all clear. Or so he thought. Gunshots appeared and echoed through the hallways. "GO, GO, GO!!" Harris orders his men to get the hostages and Fladir. His capture is part of the mission, but the priority is to get his team out. They split into two, three men going left, three right, the three right soon became 2 as one of his men stepped on a grenade, he knew if he was to move the whole building would go up. So, sacrificing himself until he got the clear would then attempt to run and jump from the building.

Harris and Fowler had made it to the centre of the building and got the message through the earpiece that Delta team had located Fladir and would extract. Beating down the door they found Hallie and Doctor Hague, only it was Hallie that was the only one left alive. They had murdered Doctor Hague. Hallie was beaten and unconscious on the floor beside Doctor Hague. Both Harris and Fowler expected the worse, when they went over to her, she still had a pulse. "We need to get her out of here now!" Fowler demanded as he moved his gun to his back and picked Hallie up.

"Fowler." Harris had shouted and when Fowler had turned around, he was stood still, frozen. He had been shot. Fowler hoisted Hallie to his shoulder, pulled his gun around and shot the man behind Harris. Hurrying over to Harris, Fowler offered his arm, but Harris declined and placed his hand to his stomach where you could see the blood. "I don't give a shit if you out rank me Harris, get your fucking arm around me and help me get Jones out of here alive. Now!" Fowler's demand seemed to work as Harris was limping out using Fowler as support to walk. Three army lorries were waiting out front for arrival of the extraction and then a loud BANG! The whole place went up just as they were driving off. The last thing heard through the earpiece was all special force team who entered other than Harris and Fowler died before the building blew up.

The hospital was full of casualties from that mission but had some of the best doctors and medics you have ever seen. Hallie was still not awake but stable, Harris's doctor gave Fowler a look that it was not looking good.

"Harris, hey. How are you doing?" Fowler asked in a quiet tone, he already knew the answer but needed Harris to keep talking.

"Shit," the more Harris coughed the more blood came up. "I know I'm not going back home alive." Those words hit Fowler hard, in a way he wanted to convince Harris they were not true. But he knew they were.

"But you're coming home regardless, we got you out."

"No mate, you got me out. Thanks to you I won't rot in this hell hole but in my own country." More blood was coming out of his mouth.

"Harris, I..." No words could describe this. Fowler was watching his best friend die and had to witness the one woman who he had deep feelings for not wake up because she was beaten so badly. All he wanted to do was kill Fladir and all his sick army. This was not the time for vengeance.

"Don't worry mate. How is Hallie?" Even on his death bed he cared.

"She's stable, beaten pretty bad but doc says she put up a bloody good fight."

"Trained her well, I think. I know we were all close, but I see the way you look at Hallie, you need to make a move before you lose her to someone else. Just know, even if I'm dying, you break her heart I'll come and haunt you." Harris began to laugh before coughing up some more blood.

"I would never, you know me to well for that. Just never thought I'd lose you?"

"Just promise me you will look after Hallie, no matter what. We both have no family, no one to call. This place was my family and always will be." The look Harris gave Fowler he knew time was limited.

"I promise." Fowler had kept back his tears. He wasn't an emotional type, but this hurt. Hurt bad.

"Harris, Harris? Doctor quick, doctor help us." Fowler was shouting and the doctors were doing all they could to revive Harris, but no pulse came back. He was gone

12

"Excuse me?" Mrs. Wilson asked as for the first time since this discussion began all eyes were on Hallie.

"James Wilson, he might go under a different name now but was known as James as a child. Any ideas?" Hallie knew she had their full attention now.

"N-no, I'm sorry detectives, you must be mistaken. We know no one of that name nor did our Katie." Judge Wilson responded with certainty, however Mrs. Wilson not so much. You could see the unease of the situation written across her face. Both Hallie and Fowler were good at getting a reaction from people and getting the truth.

"Okay, well you both just had the biggest opportunity to tell us the truth but instead chose not to. You see we know who James is and his relation to you." Hallie stood her ground and was pissed off. Still professional but pissed."

"Are calling me a liar. In my own home!" Many people heard judge Wilson raise his voice, this was a defensive tone to scare people off but, it would take a lot to scare these two off.

"Not at all, sir," Hallie didn't want to say his name, sir was professional and for her to remember her job and not lash out, sir seemed appropriate. "What I want to know is how you have kept a lie so buried all these years that when you know as well as I do who he is and was to you both. So, we came here to hear this from your mouth, your words. Who is he? Cause we can dig and keep on digging and whatever we come back with might not look pretty! James had communications with Katie so we need all information on James as you can tell us cause for all we know he could've been the last one to see her or know who killed her." Fowler kept his eye contact firmly on both Wilson, he read reactions well and knew if he needed to jump in, he could.

"Rob, we can tell them. They already know." Mrs. Wilson whispered to Judge Wilson. "You both may want to sit back down."

Relief, Hallie and Fowler made some progress. Little but still progress.

"James was two years older than Katie. He adored her, loved her so much was such an amazing big brother until the accident." Mrs. Wilson stuttered on the word accident, this many years later and still couldn't talk about it.

"What accident?" Hallie seemed less pissed off now she was getting the truth. More consoling in her words.

"We knew James was different. He was a premature baby and throughout a young age his mind just worked differently. He struggled some days knowing Katie needed our attention as well as he did. Sharing wasn't a strong suit of his." Mrs. Wilson was defending his actions and spoke in a manner of forgiveness.

"Don't defend him Ann. He tried to kill her. He knew what he was doing." Judge Wilson spat; anger filled the room.

"He was a child Robert. A child, and a troubled on, it was our fault for not watching them both." This was the first time Mrs. Wilson raised her voice and stood to take higher ground.

"It wasn't our fault, you know it. He wasn't right in the head."

"Okay, how about we stop pointing fingers and figure out how Katie knew him now? Any ideas if Katie mentioned any new friends or new names?" Hallie knew this argument was going to happen, but she was running out of time.

"I mean no new names, she spoke about people at the hospital, but people on the outside was Alex, Parker, Juliet and Nathan."

Both Hallie and Fowler looked at each other. Nathan was a common name, but the previous person convicted for these killings was Nathan.

"Would you know of all their surnames and where we could find Nathan and Juliet?" Hallie kept composure. This could just be a coincidence.

"Yes of course. Juliet Hazelgrove, been best friends with Katie since we moved here, and Nathan's is... I don't think Katie ever told us. He had been friends with Alex and Parker first I believe?"

"Thank you, if we have anything further, we will contact you." As Hallie and Fowler began to leave Judge Wilson called for them both.

"Detectives?"

"Yes sir?"

"I apologies, for earlier, we had buried that lie for a long time. Before we moved here and put James in that hospital, we told all close family and friends he had passed away. Beyond disgraced in him and want no contact with him whatsoever."

"I understand that sir, but at this rate the two victims that have been murdered and one is a close family member of yourself and her boyfriend who you considered family. We will keep both you and your wife under security. Just in case." Hallie didn't imply that the killer was after the judge, but also expected revenge was in order.

Arriving back at the station both Hallie and Fowler are called to IT department. Hoping Gibb has a location for this James person but is something unexpected. Both Gibb and the Sergeant are awaiting the detective's arrival.

"Detectives, any luck." Sergeant already knew the answer but needed to hear it from them.

"Yes sir, they had a son. Told all their relatives and friends he died when in fact they sent him to a mental hospital because he tried to kill Katie when she was a baby."

"Shit!" Gibb realised what he said as both detectives and the Sergeant were now all staring at him. "Uhh, sorry I'll just" pointing back to his computer and began typing some coding. Fowler chuckled but continued Hallie's conversation, "two guesses to which hospital they chose for their son?"

"St Catherine's?" Sergeant knew something was different about them years ago and this just proves his theory.

"Bingo, anyways Gibb, you found where this mystery man is?"

"Still on that, the team are getting an IP address as we speak. That wasn't the reason I asked you here. I found some disturbing images on Alex's laptop." Gibb linked the laptop to the tv screen with the photos displayed.

"Is that?"

I'd Kill For You

"Katie, was Alex... stalking her?" Hallie was questioning and wanted to look away. Both Sergeant and Fowler looked away at one image which was of Katie completely naked.

"Well, that's what I thought at first,"" Gibb went on clearing his throat, "But look who comes to join her in the video."

"There is a video, what were they doing making a porno?" Fowler added still looking away.

"Wait, pause it. Look"

"Hal, no offense but if I wanted to watch people having sex, I'd watch porn, these two are dead, kind of creepy." Fowler wasn't a squeamish person but wasn't enjoying this.

"Will you both just look. It is a reflection. They were both being stalked, but the killer just gave us a reflection of him and,"

"But the stalker is in all black, can't see shit Hal?"

"I know that, but look, in a black t-shirt with a forearm tattoo. Get a screen shot of that tattoo Gibb, see if you can get out what it is."

"Yes ma'am" Gibb was straight to work pulling the image of the blurry smudge tattoo to get a clearer image.

"If we can get the image of that tattoo, could help us narrow down who this stalker is. Sir, I want to get Doctor Parker in for questioning. If he was part of the friendship group, he could be targeted but he knew Katie before Alex did, maybe a jealous tendency there and if he works at the same hospital, he has access to files and would know who Katie is long before he says he did."

"Yes, do what you must. I need this wrapped up. This killer is playing a game, a fucking hard one. In the next few days, we will get the media on our tails, we need to give them something."

"If we can get a clear view of the tattoo they can have it, the artist or friends of the stalker would've noticed it."

"It's done." Gibbs adding the image before and after to the screen.

"It's a..."

"But why"

The tattoo was of a snake wrapping around a wrist looking like it was slithering up the arm.

"I will get it clearer image in case it needs to sent to the media."

"Thank you Gibb, right lets head ba..." Before Fowler could continue a chanting noise was coming from Alex's laptop. A notification went to the Sergeant's phone alerting of an email.

"The laptop, its completely shut down, I will get it hooked up and all data sent over."

"Thank you Gibb, killer must still have access to it, shut it down remotely. Sir, is everything okay."

"Yes, it is fine, meeting in an hour. Are you both okay with this? Keep me in the loop."

"Yes sir."

As Gibb began the encryption on Alex's laptop, he assured him he would keep the detectives in the loop. No need to wait as could take a while. Hallie knew this was the time to go back to the office and go through all evidence they have.

13

"Detective, I need you both to come to the lab."

"We are on route back to the station can swing through after?" Fowler has his phone on speaker through his car with Hallie focusing on the notes of this case.

"Need you here now really, this cannot wait." Jameson was the one person to make light on all things no matter how horrible the situation is.

"Jameson, it's Hallie, what's going on?" Least with Hallie talking they might get an answer.

"Well, your voice is always a delight. But I have been advised to not give any information over the phone. It is something we have found."

Fowler looked over to Hallie to see her smirking, he soon grabbed Hallie's leg and squeezed tightly with a look on his face that meant Hallie was his and his alone.

"We will be right there." Fowler ended the call and turned straight to Hallie, whilst driving on his hand still firmly grasping Hallie's leg. Fowler began to speed up not making eye contact with Hallie.

"What was that look for?"

"You know what Jameson is like Hal, no need to entertain it."

"Okay, let's get one thing straight right now." Hallie's tone was stern, she was not happy, she brushed Fowler's hand off her leg and moved herself in the chair so she was now facing Fowler. "If I wanted to pursue something with Jameson, believe me I would've done it by now. Have I entertained something to make him think he has a chance, no. And finally, you do not talk to me like I am a piece of shit you find on the side of the road." Once Hallie had finished her rant, they had pulled up at forensics.

"Hal, wait."

"Don't bother." Already slamming the door on Fowler Hallie began walking into the building, Fowler keeping close by.

"Hallie, please."

"This is not the time nor the place Adam."

As both enter the lab both Katie and Alex's dead bodies lay on the autopsy boards. They look peaceful but they both knew that they endured torture before taking their last breath.

"Jameson, what you found?" Hallie turning away from Fowler to take her mind off what happened in the car.

"Ahh detectives, that suit really makes your ass look good Fowler." Usually, Jameson complements Hallie but proving Hallie's argument that it wasn't flirting made her smile.

"Have I missed something?" Jameson looks between both detectives in confusion wondering if something was mentioned he should know about.

"Nothing important, what you found?"

"Well, both victims were poisoned by the same drug. A drug specifically used to help ease people or help them sleep. These two were injected with this and looking at it, near around the same time."

"Wait, so they were drugged together but killed separately."

"Precisely, I assume the killer wants to play some game. Torture is the word to describe this."

"Okay, can you give me a copy of what you have found all on paper, avoiding emails like the plague at the moment." Hallie looked over to Fowler who was still looking as pissed off as before which gave Hallie a sense of happiness knowing she was in the right.

"Of course, was briefed on that, one more thing you need. I'm no IT expert but I know for a fact this is not in the human anatomy." Jameson handed over a clear package with a USB drive inside. Found this inside one of the victims, must've swallowed it before being drugged."

"How can you be so sure the killer didn't make them swallow it whilst drug, another trick wouldn't surprise me." Fowler still pissed off but making sense.

"Because the drug used was injected into them and once in the system it is like you would just be asleep like in a coma until woken by another drug to which they were tortured not long after I'd say. Only way to find out if it was to find out what is on it." Jameson handed the USB over to Hallie and looked both Hallie and Fowler up and down. "I know it isn't my place detectives, but you both look like shit, have you even slept?"

"In all honesty, no we haven't. Thank you, keep us informed if you find anything else."

"Will do."

Fowler made sure no one was around before getting back into his car with Hallie. Hallie wanted to find out what was on the USB, Fowler did too, but he wanted to make sure they were on good terms.

"Hal, can we talk?"

"We can, later. We need to sort this out first."

"I know. Your right, work first."

All Hallie wanted right now was the comfort of Fowler, but she was stubborn and held her ground well. Soon after Hallie rang Gibb pre warning him about this USB stick and that they will be in the office in 5 minutes.

"Well, it is a good job I was able to complete the last job you gave me before getting this. What is it by the way?"

"We don't know Gibb, forensics gave it to us, found in one of the victims' bodies."

"Okay, you could've told me that BEFORE you let me touch it!" Gibb looking horrified he has just touched something which was inside someone.

"Oh relax, they cleaned what they could." Fowler looking over to Hallie knowing this may not be true.

"Okay let's plug it in see what can find." Surprisingly it worked which was shocking knowing where it had been. It contained files of images, videos, and documents which all looked like normal things, why was it in Alex's stomach. "I'll do some digging, see what they had to hide so much he had to swallow it." Still squirmiest at the thought it was inside someone made both Hallie and Fowler laugh.

"Thank you, Gibb." As Fowler was about to leave Hallie stopped in her tracks,

"Gibb, you said you completed something else, what was it?"

"Oh yeah, that phone of the first victim, the person who's contact didn't have name just a question mark. I found where the phone was last used, but the phone hasn't been used since the 24th of February."

"24th February, that was the day you got them emails from Katie laptop." Hallie began to look concerned.

"Indeed, that isn't the worse of it."

"Go on?"

"The IP address shows that it was last used here. In this building." Gibb now sharing the concern. He knew this was serious. However, this is something else. This contact was in the building when the email came through, that contact was in connection with Katie, saved in her contacts. All the pieces, now both Hallie and Fowler needed to put them together.

14

Back in the office, Hallie and Fowler begin going through all the evidence. Anything they could have missed earlier and adding to potential suspects.

Parker Fields-
- History with Alex before they met Katie.
- Has a photo of Katie on his desk even though she was with Alex?
- Pretended to not know Alex last name when they studied together.
- Gave a grey file of all Katie info in willingly.
- Met Katie's parents.
- Got her working in the same building as himself.

Juliet Hazelgrove
- Katie's best friend
- Lives in Dubai with her fiancée
- Has an alibi as is due to give birth any day so on a no-fly list?
- Last in contact with Katie- 23rd February- day before her death
- Also didn't know a Nathan as never met him only Alex and Parker

Nathan
- Mystery man- no one knew of his last name and was waiting for Parkers arrival to the station for questioning.

- No photos of him on either Katie or Alex phone
- Heard of Nathan through Katie's parents
- Previous convict was named Nathan Smith
- Could this be the mystery contact in Katie's phone?
- Police has located a address linked from the IP address from Katie's contact list and derelict house, no furniture nothing.

Judge Wilson and Mrs. Wilson
- Both Hallie and Fowler knew they weren't the killer, but they had lied to them about their son. What else would they hide?

James Wilson
- Another mystery man.
- Was admitted to St Catherine's Hospital at 6 years of age.
- The family cut ties with him and told Katie he wasn't real.
- Katie knew of him and wanted to find him?
- Could be jealous, kill Katie and her boyfriend to have his parents back and to himself again?

Both Hallie and Fowler are deep in the case files, going through the old case and this case to see if any links, any muck ups from the killer that they could use. Anything really to get a decent lead to who the killer is.

"Detectives, we have Parker Fields in interrogation room three" PC Gardener entered the room as both Hallie and Fowler were deep in thought.

"Thank you, we will be right there." Waiting for PC Gardener to leave Hallie looks over to Fowler about to say something about them but refrains. "Let's find out why this fucker is lying too. I'm sure no one wants to tell the truth the first time now days."

"I think you're right about that. After you." As Fowler held the door open for Hallie, they walked down the long corridor barely saying two words to each other. Just about to head into the interrogation room Fowler pulls Hallie aside to an empty meeting room, closes the door and uses his body to stop anyone getting in or Hallie getting out.

"What you…"

"Hallie, this, us, I refuse to carry on life working with you if every day will be like today and get the silent treatment."

"Wow, you really are great at your timings Adam!"

"I'm serious. Talk to me. I know we have a case to solve, and this fucker isn't an easy one but last night?"

"Last night was amazing, but we both are new to this. We work together and need to remember that. Can we do this later please. I want to get this out the way."

No response, Fowler moves to open the door gesturing Hallie to go first, and both headed into the interrogation room.

"Hello Parker, thank you for coming here I know it's late."

"Of course, Detective, anything I can do to be of help."

Fowler took the reins; Hallie knew to jump in when needed but let Fowler take the lead on this one. "You see Parker, nearly every person involved with this case has lied to us. Including you."

"I. Me? I don't understand."

"Oh, I'm sure you don't but let me paint the picture for you. You see, we know you knew Alex before Katie, we also know it was you who introduced Katie to Alex. What we don't understand is why you would lie to us about not knowing who he is?"

Hallie remained silent but alert, reading Parkers facial expression.

"I shouldn't of okay. I know I shouldn't of, but we were no longer friends me and Alex, not since the holiday to the mountains." Parker didn't make eye contact but looked down at his hands rubbing his fingers together. Hallie noticed he had scratches on his hand which he soon covered after looking down.

"Why since the holiday. We know Alex didn't want Katie going, why was that?"

"Because it was an anonymous donation from someone to the hospital staff on level 5. For taking so much care and compassion with the patients. We assumed it was from one of the patient's parents as most of them were rich. Anyway, Alex was worried that Katie would be in danger and didn't want her going. I volunteered to go just to look after Katie, I didn't want to go but done it for them."

Fowler introjected, "You didn't want to go on a free holiday to the mountains with one of your so-called best friends?"

"Of course, I would go on holiday with my best friends but the mountains, its cold, snow everywhere, no thank you, if it was on a plane somewhere hot yes, please."

"Okay, so why then after the trip did you and Alex fall out. Did something happen between you and Katie?"

Parker looked up instantly in shock. "I told you both before Katie was just my friend, nothing else, nothing more just a friend." Parkers voice was raised slightly, both Fowler and Hallie are sleep deprived and not in the best of moods, Hallie began to introject.

"All we want to know is the truth. Look at it from what we are seeing, you go on a holiday with your friend's girlfriend, you have her photo on your desk, you lied about knowing Alex, and now you are raising your voice at us for asking questions?"

"I'm sorry, but to answer again, nothing I mean nothing ever happened between me and Katie. I'm not attracted to... that... you know.... Gender."

Fowler looked over to Hallie for her to continue, "so you are attracted to men only not females?"

"Yes, I am.... Well gay." Parker kept delaying the end of his sentences like he was about to be judged by both detectives.

"Okay, makes sense now. What still doesn't make sense is why you and Alex had a falling out?" Hallie began to think if this was going to be helpful information or a confession?

"The day before we were about to return, Katie got a call from Alex saying he felt like he was being watched and uncomfortable around one of my friends. Well, ex friends now. But as we got home Alex accused him of being a stalker and knowing loads about him and Katie and they're too privileged and got the dream life. Well, I spoke with him, you know, asked his opinion and he said he did nothing of the sort. Well, I stupidly believed him which cost my friendship with both Alex and Katie. Katie was more forgiving as I still had to see her everyday but wasn't the same."

"Who is this friend Parker" Fowler leaning forward intrigued by his answer.

"His name is Nathan Smith."

"Are you still in contact with him Parker?" Fowler adding caution to the questions to not make Parker suspect anything.

"I haven't spoken to him since beginning of Feb, he was acting weird then asked about Alex and Katie, lead me to believe they were right all along so I cut him off. He did text me out the blue few days ago thinking about it. I ignored it."

"What did the message say?"

"Here you read it, I left it on unread, wanted him to think I blocked him."

Hallie looked on the table and read the message aloud,

'Glad to know you used me just as much. I gave you plenty of signs I wasn't interested in you that way and you do that. Sick'

"Parker, what was Nathan's address for me?"

"I don't know, we only met a few months ago, he said he lived in Salisbury at his aunt's house which I never went to. I should have just asked."

"How did you both meet?" Hallie needed as much information from Parker as possible to track him down. If he was just using Parker than he could be the killer?

"Met him down The White Horse, it is a pub on West View Road. Went after a hard shift for a drink and bite to eat, he approached me, we hit it off. I mean who wouldn't he was so handsome and didn't know if he was gay."

"And was he?"

"No, but I enjoyed knowing I could be friend someone that looked that good."

"Do you have a photo of him?"

"No, tried to get one sneakily once but didn't work. He never took any photos with me says he wanted to live in the moment hated technology, had a shitty phone just text and call no camera, Internet nothing. That should have been red flag number 1."

It was getting late, but they finally had a description of mystery man, now to get one of the artists to draw it out and have an image of him.

15

Going through the data base with the lead of Nathan Smith as prime suspect, finally having a photo of him to go by Hallie and Fowler began by attempting to log last where abouts, checking CCTV footage from the day both victims were found, running all necessary background checks, previous work places- all fake, house in Salisbury- lies, but the more Hallie stared at this man's image, the more she felt like she had seen him somewhere.

"Everything alright Hal?" Fowler could see she was deep in thought but confusion on her face.

"I just, I feel like I have seen him before. Get them to run a check on his face to see if he matches anyone that has come in the station, maybe arrested. I could just be over-thinking it."

"Better to be over cautious in this case. Look it's 11pm, how about call it a night and crack on with this in the morning. Do you want me to drive you home?" Fowler wanted to be with Hallie, spend as much time as he could with her, but work took priority, he knows that.

"That's okay, I'll take one of the cars and see you here in the morning."

"Of course, I'll see you in the morning Hal, make sure you get some rest."

Hallie knew if Fowler took her home, she would end up back in the same situation as the night before. Rest is what she needed, and taking herself home was the right thing to do.

As Hallie arrived back at her flat, she walked past her hallway mirror, took a quick glance at herself an realised she really did look like shit. Heavy bags under her eyes from lack of sleep, hair in a messy bun beyond saving and clothes she had worn two days straight, a shower and glass of wine was in order.

Jumping straight into bed, wine in one hand and tv remote in the other at least Hallie felt a bit more human after her shower. Her towel dried hair covered her shoulders and began to dampen her over-sized baggy t-shirt which just made it to the top of her thighs in length. One thing she hadn't done was look at her phone, kept on glancing over to see if she had a message but nothing. It was best that Fowler didn't message, maybe he took Hallie's advice and put work first. But Hallie was over thinking the situation. Since that night, as she lay in her king size bed alone, no one wants to be alone. Hallie had been alone her whole life and Fowler cared for her since she was 16. Missing his warmth in bed and his chat, Hallie reaches for her phone, gets Fowler's name up in contacts and messages him.

'Hey, sorry I know it's late. You still awake?"

Awaiting a response felt like a lifetime but then saw the 3 little dots showing Fowler was typing.

"Always awake, are you okay?"

Relief spread across Hallie; she intently gained the butterflies back in her stomach. She never had feelings for someone before. Knowing she needed to make sure work was first, she just needed someone. Not just anyone, but him.

"We never did have that chat properly, just thinking about it now."
…
"You're right, I'm sorry. I got slightly protective."
…
"Slightly??? Maybe a bit more than slightly Adam."
…
"I agree, I have cared about you for as long as I have known you Hal, now I have you just don't want to lose you."

A huge smile rose across Hallie's face. No one has ever wanted her, not in that way. She had dates and other hook ups but that was to fill a need. This felt different and she didn't want to lose it either.

"I care a lot for you too Adam. But work needs to be our priority. It fucking sucks I know that but must be that way till case is closed and we find this killer. Then can come out into the open."

...

"I agree. Sooner we catch this killer the better for everyone."

...

"Indeed. Just so you know Adam, I care a lot about you and have done for a while."

...

"Thats a relief. Least we on the same page."

...

"I'm glad."

...

"So, what you doing then Hal?"

...

"Led on my bed, you?"

...

"At your front door"

Hallie went straight to her doorbell app to check the camera. It is true, he was stood there, soaking wet as was chucking it down outside so must've been the run from his car to the door. Hallie went straight to the door, took off the door chain, unlocked the bolt and opened it. Gazing up to Fowler, he grabbed her and kissed her, picking her up and carrying her indoors kicking the door closed with his foot. Hallie knew what she wanted, and Fowler was giving it to her. Fowler drops Hallie on her bed, and both begin to undress each other, Fowler began kissing down Hallie's neck, lowering himself down her body Hallie sat up in line with Fowler's chest.

Clothes lay scattered across the floor, Hallie knew this was a bad idea, they were supposed to be slowing down to focus on the case, but this was a lot harder than she thought. Fowler had Hallie in a tight grip led on top of her, with every movement he knew he had her just where he wanted her. Hallie reached for the bed sheets and gripped them tightly with both hands to then quickly wrapped her arms around Fowler's broad back, nails digging into his skin as she pulled her hands up his back to wrap around his neck. Fowler grabbed both of Hallie's arms and pinned them down on the bed and began kissing her neck. Both had dominance but it was Fowler who made sure he had Hallie in line and begging him for more.

16

10 years ago

The sound of hospital monitors beeping around, Hallie slowly opens her eyes and at first everything was a blur. It took a few blinks for everything to come into focus, the last Hallie remembers is being beaten by terrorist for not disclosing any information on her team. Everything is coming into focus, the white hospital gown and a blue blanket covering Hallie to her waist. Taking everything in she could she looks to her left, monitors that she was hooked up too beeping away, to her right is Adam Fowler asleep on the hospital chair. Bruises over his face, cuts also one deep enough it will scar his face across his cheek. "Adam?" Hallie groaned, this felt like a dream she thought she would never get out of there alive.

"Hey, hey you. How are you feeling?" Fowler shot up out of his chair to lean to Hallie and grabbed her by the hand and kissed it. "So glad your awake, I'm going to go get a doctor," but as Fowler stood up to go get a doctor, Hallie squeezed his hand as tight as she could to get his attention,

"No… no please don't leave me alone. Please?" Hallie was holding back the tears; she was still petrified and who could blame her.

"It's okay, hey look at me, you are safe, and I am never going to leave you again, you hear me. Come here." Fowler made room next to Hallie on her bed to hug her. She felt safe in his arms but couldn't hold back the tears. So many emotions and feelings rushing through Hallie, not to mention being in pain from broken ribs, broken wrist from being tied up too tight and severe concussion. Fowler reached down to get the buzzer so a doctor could come in without him having to leave Hallie. "Hal, do you know where you are?" his words were soft as he stroked Hallie's hair for comfort still arms wrapped around her. Her head lay on Fowler's chest, she didn't want to move just in case it wasn't real.

"In hospital I guess, unless this is a dream which is why I don't want you to leave."

"It isn't a dream Hal, you are in hospital, we got you out."

"Just doesn't seem real, I didn't think I was ever going to get out."

"Well, you are out and safe,"

"How long have I been here?"

"Only for a few hours over night. We got lots to talk about Hal, but a doctor needs to check you out first, need the all clear before."

"Before what?" Hallie lifted her head off Fowler's chest and looked him square in the eyes. "Before what, Adam?"

Three knocks at the door and two doctors and a nurse walk in. "I'm sorry to interrupt but we saw the buzz, ahh Hallie you're awake. How are you feeling?" The doctor was a tall man who was Arabic he had perfect straight teeth and a kind gentle smile. Fowler lifted himself off the bed and back to the chair he had been sleeping on, but Hallie followed him with her eyes, as soon as Fowler had sat down, they both made eye contact and he reached for her hand.

"Urm, well I'm alive so guess that's a bonus." Hallie attempted to joke just to ease the tension. This was something she had always done especially with strangers.

"That is very true, Hallie. We need to run some tests on you now you are awake Miss Jones and I know your superiors would like a chat with you, but I have already told them they are not to see you till you are ready, okay?"

Hallie felt relief, the longer she could put off the torture she endured over the past few days which felt like a lifetime for her, the better. "Yes of course. Can Fowler stay though please?"

"Long as you want me here love, I'm staying." Fowler had a small smile rise and his face was just in relief that Hallie was alive.

"Of course, there are a few things we need to check first like your wounds, Lance Corporal Fowler would need to stand outside the room but can come straight back I assure you." Hallie looked and nodded to

Fowler that this was okay. Fowler squeezed Hallie's hand slightly stood up and went to wait outside.

"Is she awake?" Captain Brooks was special forces commanding officer. A tall, big build, however in his mid-forties he was close to retirement. His days out on field were limited hence his title and ranking.

"She is sir." Fowler stood up as quick as he could without showing he was in any pain.

"And? How is she?"

"She is stable, alert, knows who she is, who I am but is, she's hurt sir, mentally and physically. Sustained broken ribs, a broken wrist and concussion by them bastards and is traumatized, she didn't want me to leave. I have never, never in my years seen Hallie cry. Not even in the tear gas mission,"

"Yeah, she really showed all you boys up on that one!" The captain guided Fowler to sit down, and he joined him.

"As soon as she said my name when she woke up, my whole stomach just erupted. I was so happy to see her, awake. But when I said to go get a doctor for her, she begged me not to leave her alone, she cried on me. Not only broke me but feels like, I knew sir. I knew in my gut not to let her go in that fucking ambulance, but I did."

"You can't change the past Fowler, you know that. It was a call and she's one stubborn woman, she always has been she would've gone even if you or Harris told her no."

"I haven't told her anything sir or asked her anything about what happened."

"No, best not yet anyways. Let her get the all clear from doctors first then need to find out exactly what they done or said to her. And you, no offense Fowler you look like shit." Captain nudged Fowler to try get him to smile which it worked in some way.

"I feel it sir."

"Well, least you are doing okay, stitches in the face too, nasty one there, you'll end up having a scar like me." Captain pointed to back of his head where he had a large white scar from a previous mission. One of the doctors emerged out of Hallie's room and looked at both Fowler and the captain.

"Well, it is a good job she has a high pain tolerance. Any normal person would've screamed or even punched me for that. Looks like she will recover well, no long-term problems that I can see. Will do a head CT later today just to check for any swellings or brain bleeds/bruising. She is ready to talk when you need her though Captain."

"Thank you, come on then." Both entered Hallie's room to see her sat up right in bed. Uncomfortable but a forced smile appeared. "You're not fooling me Jones, even as your captain you can relax."

"Yes sir, good to see you."

"And you, all were worried about you, but we knew we'd find ya."

Hallie looked to Fowler than back at Captain, she knew they wanted to know what happened and sooner she told them the sooner she could block it out of her memory.

Fowler went to Hallie's side and knelt beside her, "Hal, you know if you're not ready to talk about what happened, that's okay."

"I know, the sooner I tell you about it though the sooner I can learn to forget about it." Hallie said looking down at her hand which was bandaged up. She was trying her hardest to keep herself composed in front of both Fowler and Captain to which she realised she was missing someone.

"Where is Harris?"

Fowler looked up to Captain as he knew this was going to be hard for Hallie to hear.

"Hallie, I need to grab a couple of my colleagues before you begin about what happened when you were taken okay, I'll be right back, Fowler will be here. Won't be long." Captain nodded at Fowler to give him the go ahead as to what happened on the rescue mission and left the room dialling on his phone.

"Adam, what happened? I know that nod, I have been on the receiving end of that nod. Where is Harris." Hallie sat herself up as Fowler took her hand that wasn't in a bandage.

"Hal, we had a rescue mission to get you and the doctor out. It was our team, special forces, and delta team. It was a clear extraction, we learned the blueprints of the building, got the best people on the mission as we had intelligence that Fladhir was in the same building due to it being heavily guarded. Our team split up to cover more ground, me, Harris, and Felix. Felix stepped on a hidden trigger, he knew if he moved it would detonate and no idea where. Harris and I came looking for you, the building was full of Fladhir's men. When we found you, the doctor was already dead, you close to being. I lifted you over my shoulders and carried you out but Harris, he was shot and shot badly. I managed to get you both out, Harris was shot a fair number of times, and one hit went through his liver and he bled internally. He died on route Hal, I'm so sorry." Fowler was tearing up but kept composure but didn't look Hallie in the eye.

"Adam, look at me." Fowler's eyes lifted to meet Hallie's and she rested her hand on his cheek. "You saved us both, I couldn't thank you enough. Harris was a close friend to both of us. Well, he was really the only family I ever had. But it wasn't your fault."

Hallie brought Fowler in for a hug, and she squeezed him as tight as she could. Tears rolling down her cheek but knowing his body will be able to come home was enough.

The door to Hallie's room opened a jar and Captain peered his head through and cleared his throat. Hallie let go of Fowler and dried her eyes and Fowler stood at attention.

"At ease to you both, you both been to hell and back, you are off duty now, okay?"

"Yes sir."

"Good, Jones, Fowler, this is Chief Zhung and Chief Kolby both here with me just to take notes and brief their teams who are also now on this mission."

"Finally good to put a name to your heroic names. We have heard many great things about you both and your team." Chief Chung was a petite lady who was very high in rankings. Jet black hair, dark brown eyes but looked so good for her age and she had achieved many great things.

"Thank you, ma'am." Fowler said and Hallie nodded in agreement.

"Right, Jones, you are sure you're ready." Captain looked down at Hallie as she adjusted her position.

"No but fuck it." Hallie looked over to Fowler and he smirked but reassured her with his eyes, he was going nowhere.

"Okay, let's start from the beginning, when it went radio silent,"

"I knew something was wrong when the van just stopped, I assumed the drivers had a reason but looking through the peep hole we were surrounded by trucks, this is when I radioed through saying the vehicle was about to be hi-jacked. Gave the rough location and duration we had been on the road and informed would-be MIA on the radio as they had shot the drivers. I was in uniform and had no time to get out of it, I hid my gun down my back and my knife in my bra, any way to hide any weapons. Told Ashira to do the same. The back doors flew open, and the sun was so bright, took a few seconds for my eyes to adjust. At first, I thought they just wanted the patient as they dragged him out first, loaded him into a van which sped off but then they came back. I shot two and told Ashira to run and stay close. We were making some distance, ran through alley ways, dodging anything we could until Ashira fell. I went back to help her up when I was hit over the head and a grain bag went over my head. I couldn't see anything. I was chucked into a van and kicked for making any movements. So, I called for Ashira and heard her scream my name, told her to just try stay as calm as possible when I was kicked in my ribs again.

We were both carried into this building, tied up so tightly that my chest felt tight. It was... hard to breathe. The bags finally came off our heads. Ashira had a busted lip and a black eye but was awake. I asked them what they wanted with us, but they were talking in another language. Until one man walked in. Soon as I laid my eyes on him, I wanted to just shoot him. Fladhir asked why we had one of his men. I told him, he was injured, we were taking him to a hospital for treatment but if I knew it was one of his men, I would've left him there to rot. I knew I'd get beaten for that but was worth it seeing his smug face change.

We were left tied up for days. Minimal food or water. It felt like a lifetime and became weak, just left my body hang so my eyes could close just for a second, when his guard thought every time I fell asleep he would use me as a punching bag. Prick. I had training for this, I knew I would survive this if I didn't give in. It wasn't until they caught on to this."

A brief pause was there, Hallie knew she had to continue but what they were about to hear was unexpected.

"They un-tied the both of us, gave us both a cup of water and a slice of bread. I didn't give a fuck what they had done to it I had it and was gone in seconds. Wondering if they had given up, few minutes later about 7 or 8 men came in grabbing me and Ashira from the ground. I put up a fight as much as I could but was tied to a chair and a rag tied around my mouth to stop me from making a noise. They also done the same to Ashira but soon took the rags from both of our mouths. Fladhir came in and another man who was wearing a balaclava, he sat in the corner. Fladhir asked me about the team, the base anything he could about us, I wouldn't give in. No matter how much his men tried beating it out of me. Then the man who came in with Fladhir spoke up, said time to force it out of her. He had an American accent. He... I'm sorry." Hallie's voice broke and Fowler came to her side, grabbed her hand to just be there for her.

"It's okay Jones, you're doing amazing, just take your time." Chief Zhung spoke calmly with empathy knowing this was a hard thing to even listen to.

"They killed Ashira, right in front of me. Tortured her because I didn't talk or say anything about the base or our mission. She just sat there, still tied up, lifeless. She had screamed right till she took her last breath. The American then came to me and whispered in my ear. His voice was low but chilling like every word went through my body and froze me. He grabbed my hair, pulled it back and looked me dead in the eyes. "You were trained well but she could've survived if you just spoke up." Them words, he kept calling me the killer and then untied me and made me stand. I fell to the ground first, I forced myself up. He kicked me back down. This happened a good 5 times before I was on the floor and he was standing on my wrist, pushing down through his foot with all weight. You could hear it snap. It was Fladhir who shouted stop to him. He crouched done to me, grabbed me by my hair and said he'd be back for more before slamming my head against the concrete floor. From then, I remember waking up here."

Silence filled the room. Even the note taker was in shock. Fowler was looking down at Hallie's arm as couldn't look in her eyes. She was in pain, and this was trauma that would stick with her for life.

17

Hallie is woken up suddenly, covered in sweat and on the verge of being in tears she realises it was just a nightmare. "Hey, hey it's okay, come here." Fowler wraps his arms around Hallie and hugs her tight slowly laying her back down. Hallie can't help but allow the tears to roll down her cheeks attempting to catch her breath back. "Do you want to talk about it?" Fowler was gently stroking through Hallie's hair but keeping his hug tight around her, so she felt safe.

"It is the same one Adam, every time. I am back there, in that place, being beaten but it is always by the one I never saw. His voice echoes through my brain and it is like, I just want to give in, I feel every hit, kick, pulse of electric being put through my body. I'm scared to close my eyes because, every time I do, I am there, trapped." Hallie tried to get the sentence out but sniffled through parts holding back from breaking down. She was exhausted and needed a rest.

"But you are not there. Okay you are with me, and I will never leave you okay. Ever. You are safe. If you want me, I'm here." Fowler took his hand to Hallie's chin to guide her face to look up to him. Hallie nodded a response and Fowler laid with her wrapped in his arms kissing her forehead and both fell asleep together.

Alarms were in sync on both Hallie and Fowler's phones. Neither wanted to move to turn them off, they both still lay wrapped in each other's arms. To their relief the phones went silent as went on an automatic snooze. Hallie groaned as she knew they needed to get up, just as she moved to get up though Fowler grabbed her pulling her back into bed. Hallie wasn't going to put up much of a fight as was happy in bed lying next to him. Until Hallie's phone began to ring, as she looked it was Gibb from IT.

"Hello?"

"Detective, sorry, I know it is early but you both need to come and see this. I got that USB you found in the victim's stomach all cleaned up and working, there is some footage on it you need to check out."

"On our way." Hanging up the call she turned to Fowler who knew already they couldn't stay.

"I'll get coffee on quick." Fowler sighed as he got up and walked to the kitchen, not to Hallie's complaints as she loved a coffee.

Arriving at the station, both Hallie and Fowler headed to Gibb's office where they were met by the Sergeant who was as clueless as both Hallie and Fowler to what Gibb had found.

"I wanted to wait for you all to be here to see this. From what it looks like it is a drive with mainly photos and one video on. Most of the photos are of Katie and Alex but the video is what needed you all to see." Gibb turns to his laptop to link it up to the TV screen to play the footage. It is St Catherine's Hospital but at night, as if someone had broken in. Whoever is filming is getting all the photos which lie down this corridor. One of each year with patients and doctors. Each looked like a plaque with a list of who was in the photo. Was like a shrine.

"Well, this is eary?" Fowler added but Hallie was fixated on the video to see if any clues would jump out, any intel, well just anything to help get them one step closer.

"Which victim was this found in Jones?"

"Was the boyfriend sir, Alex Jonoski."

"Why would he have swallowed that? Do you think the killer forced it down?"

"I'm not sure, it could be possible that this might be another clue on the killer's trail, could be a wild goose chase or could be that Alex wanted this hidden. Gibb, can you forward all of this to me please so can go through in detail each photo and who is in it?"

"Of course, I'll get prints of each one done so they won't look blurry and can…"

"Wait pause it!" Hallie interrupted "Go back just a bit, so I can see that photo please?"

Gibb re-winded the video and got a clear screen on the photo.

"Look who it is" Fowler seemed pissed that another person had lied to them.

"Isn't that?"

"It is sir, that is James Wilson, well Nathan Smith but that boy there he looks strangely familiar?" Hallie began to rack her brain as to where she knew this boy then suddenly it clicked.

"Shit"

"What Jones, who is it?" The Sergeant wasn't the one for being the most patient and it showed in the delay response Hallie was giving him.

"Look, the name is scratched out, but you can slightly make out the name. It's George Benson."

"Fuck, that was one of the victims the last time Night Stalker was going. I didn't know he was in here. I mean would explain a lot why he was the only one who didn't have a link at the time."

"Why does everything seem to link back to this fucking hospital?"

"Honestly sir, I couldn't tell you." Hallie was in shock but relieved they were getting somewhere.

Both Hallie and Fowler headed up to their office to add this information to the time stamp. The Hospital is the most common link to every death, whether it be a patient, staff, or partner of staff. The prime suspect is Katie's lost brother who goes by Nathan Smith now. Looking over the evidence Hallie skims back through the victim's photos, where they were found, their wounds, bruises, anything to see if they had a similarity. "Fowler, come look at this." Fowler dropped his paperwork immediately and walked over to Hallie and placed his head over her shoulder.

"Why was Katie the only one to be stabbed even though she was already dead from the drug used? We need to narrow it down and find where they were killed, as there was not enough blood at the scene of the crime. It's just odd, don't you think?" Looking up to Fowler realising she needed to focus but her eyes began to wonder, from his prominent jaw line, up his cheek where a dark well-trimmed beard was forming shaping his face perfectly, straight to his eyes, those piercing blue eyes. Fowler looks down to meet Hallie's eye line, keeping a straight face he lent in closer to Hallie.

"If you keep looking at me like that then I will have to do something about it." Hallie knew he meant it and it took a lot to keep her restraint. Hallie changed the subject to take her mind off it beginning to wonder. Fowler smirked at her lack of a response and turned his head to look her directly in the eye.

Hallie clears her throat and looks back at the paperwork, "Well, does it not make you think, why Katie, the only one stabbed multiple times. But drugged before, the both of them. This isn't like last time; this time feels more like a personal attack."

"It does, question is where she was stabbed as wasn't where we found her otherwise would've been more blood. That USB is still got me questioning, it was full of photos of Alex and Katie but that video, there must be something on that."

"Everything keeps leading back to that hospital and…"

Gibb enters the room out of breath from running, "Detectives, more of the video has developed, here." Handing over the USB stick Hallie takes it and plugs it into her laptop to load up the video.

The long corridor is back from what both Hallie and Fowler saw before, however a door opens into a cloak room filled with lockers. The camera spins to another person, which is Katie, and an audio begins.

"This is it, this, Al what was the code?"

"Here, I'll do it." Alex spins the dial code which is 7640 and opens the locker door. There is a photo hung on the door which looks like it has been burnt but inside, Katie places a present like box and takes away a small package.

"There you go, it's all yours." Katie looked at the camera dead in the lens as if she was looking at you, then the video cuts out.

"Time to take a trip back there I'd say." Fowler was already grabbing his keys and jacket, but Hallie hadn't moved from the screen. "Hal?"

"Yeah, sorry, that photo, I have seen it before."

"Okay, well if Gibb can get a clearer view on it than we will know for sure, right Gibb?"

"Of course, it'll be done by the time your back."

"Thank you, Hal lets go check this out see if whatever Katie put in there is still there." This came as more of a demand as Fowler was already at the door.

18

Luckily the drive from the station to St Catherine's wasn't very far, about a 15-minute drive and with Fowler driving, Hallie had time to gather her thoughts. It was a beautiful day, the sun shining, birds chirping away, the route had a lovely scenery. Fowler took a shorter route which led through country lanes, you could see a farmer ploughing his field in the distance.

Both detectives knew that this place would give them answers for many different things, however their arrival at the hospital was greeted by a familiar face, Mrs. Kirk, the receptionist who had a very different manner than the last arrival. Slouched over her desk her eye line rose, she saw them both. Mrs. Kirk sat bolt upright with a forced smile. "Detectives, urm how can I help?"

"Hello again, Mrs. Kirk, isn't it?" Hallie politely said with a soft tone.

"Uhh yes, Detective. How can I help?"

"Yes, we have a warrant to investigate the hospital so we shall leave this with you and make our way." Leaving the letter from the courts on the desk both Hallie and Fowler headed to the elevator with no questions asked. They knew where they needed to go as Alex had recorded every step with Katie. However, as the elevator doors opened the corridor that awaits is just as eery as it was on the video.

A long dark corridor on the 13th floor of St Catherine's. On the map downstairs it is shown as a staff area, history of it that this was the floor for the insane minded. The corridor showed all the same photos on the wall as it did in Alex and Katie's video, however neither Hallie or Fowler paid much attention to the photos, just to get in that room and see what is in that locker. As they both entered the room, Hallie flicked a light on which had an old bulb that flickered until it warmed up enough to stay on making a distinctive sound. Both detectives already had gloves on and a bag just in case they needed to remove anything from the room as evidence. "Okay was this locker, need to just be cautious when opening it, no idea what this killer might have left." Hallie slowly opened the locker and to her surprise wasn't booby-trapped or anything gruesome left inside. Just a note which is what Katie had put inside in the video. The killer hasn't been back yet for it. Hallie opens the letter which she read aloud whilst Fowler was checking the other 7 lockers and anything else he could find in this room.

"Here is what you asked for. Now leave us both alone, a deal is a deal!"

Hallie paused and looked up for Fowler's input. "A deal is a deal. So, they were all in connection with each other but why?"

"I have no idea but look at this!" Fowler handed over an old card to Hallie which he found under one of the old coats hanging up. The card was crumpled up and shoved in the inside coat pocket of what looked like an old trench coat.

'The Happiest of Birthdays to my special boy. I know you don't want to speak to me, but I will never forget you, my sweet pea. Here is a photo of your birth family like you asked for. But don't forget me, I loved you for who you are and no one else.

Enjoy your special day and use my gift as good use.
Love your Mumma bear.'

The envelope was stained and had marks all over it however, written on the bottom of the envelope was the sender's address. Needed something to make it out so Hallie suggested we take it back as evidence. Inside the card was still a family photo, a young boy of you had to guess was around five or six, a young girl around two/three and the parents and straight away Hallie knew these two. "Fowler, did you take a look at the photo?"

"No why?"

"Look who's faces have popped up, again!"

"The Wilson's. They really are everywhere. So, whoever wrote this letter knew their secret."

"And also told their son who they were and gave him a photo." Hallie was now sure that whoever sent this card must have something to do with it all.

"Everything keeps pinning back to this secret son of theirs. But how do we still not have a location or any information on him."

"Let's get this back to the lab, take photos of everything in this room, get forensic up here for prints see if we can get any other prints other than Katie and Alex's. The killer must have come here, like his secret hide out as this floor hasn't been used in years. I'm going to see if someone can find out who the sender of this card is. At least then we can find out who she was sending it too and how long she knew." Hallie was feeling hopeful, like she was finally one step ahead of the killer. Knowing that the killer hadn't come back here meant one thing either they beat he or she too it or Katie made a deal with someone else?

Walking back down the long corridor to head back to the elevator Hallie was looking at some of the photos when she stopped dead in her tracks and dropped her phone with the evidence bag she was carrying.

"Hal? You alright?" Fowler walked to her, but no words left her mouth, she was fixated on one of the photos that hung on the wall. Fowler looked at the photo but didn't see anything, just patients and a few doctors. There were no names on the photo like one before just people. "Hallie, kind of worrying me now. What's going on?"

Hallie goes to speak but nothing comes out, she clears her throat and points at a woman who is sat in the photo. This woman had dark curly hair, a look on her that she wasn't really there, she had two people either side of her wheelchair, but she was handcuffed to it.

"Okay, am I supposed to know who she is?" Fowler was trying to figure out who the woman was but had no idea?

"I'd hope you don't know who she is." Hallie was able to talk but her voice shaky, "That's my mother."

19

"What do you mean, I thought you was an orphan?" Fowler was confused. He knew Hallie's past, well some of it, but she never spoke about any family members even back in the army.

"I was, I ran away when I was 7 after my mother chose drugs and her abusive boyfriend over me. I was only young, but I couldn't do it." Hallie was one for being very monotone and to the point, nothing really affected her but even Fowler could see this was hitting a nerve. "She was a drug addict; she would choose drugs over anything. No idea who my real dad was, probably someone she just slept with to hit up another score. But she lost it one day, said I took up too much time, was too much, she decided to pin me down and stamp her lit cigarette into my skin, all over my arms my stomach to the point the scars are still there to this day. I knew I needed to run, so I did. A local policeman found me running and took me to the station, I wouldn't talk, they looked after me. Until they put me into a foster home. I was put in 6 homes in total. None of bad behaviour or because they didn't like me, all because it was temporary housing. I made sure I would do well out of life, I just pretended that she didn't exist so I would never have to talk about her. Hence why when I was 16, I was straight in for the army. I never knew she was in here." Silence grew, Hallie just stared at the photo and Fowler at her. Hallie's eyes had welled up during her explanation of who she was. But she didn't cry, she held it together.

"Hal, come here" Fowler opened his arms and hugged Hallie tightly. "I'm sorry, I had no idea." He rested his head on top of hers and while speaking, knowing that Hallie felt safe when with him Fowler had this sense of anger that went through him. He knew how amazing Hallie is and for someone who had a shitty life like hers and turned out amazing that anger soon dissolved.

"Thank you," she sniffled and wiped her eyes wither her sleeve. I'm taking this photo; I need more information."

"Okay, but it has to go to evidence Hallie."

"I know, and it should be evidence cause look who also there." Hallie pointed to another figure in the photo who looked familiar. A young boy sat cross legged on the floor of the photo with a young girl, but her face was scratched out the photo. The boy was James Wilson. The Wilson's secret son.

As they arrived back on the ground floor, they signed out and informed Mrs. Kirk they will be returning as will a forensic, she would need to call whoever runs the hospital to come and meet with them. Mrs. Kirk was straight on the phone and both detectives headed back to the car when they were stopped by someone calling their names.

"Dr Fields. Everything okay?" Hallie asked as she knew the answer already judging by the look on Parkers face.

"Urm, yes well no I thought you should see this." Parker took out his phone and showed them a text message.

Unknown

'Hey P, I'm sorry I blanked you and made you lose your trust in me. But you have every right to know. I wanted something that you had which I now have so thank you. Now all I will say is don't deceive me or you'll get it too. But I'm sure you won't. You've been good to me this far. Anyways, enjoy your life and hope you make some new friends, maybe ones that won't use you like they did and like you did with me. See you around. N'

"N, is that short for Nathan?" Hallie looked up from the phone first and straight to Parker.

"Yes, we would never use full names just N and P for each other. Was easier. But I tried to text back, and it wouldn't send."

"Parker, can you come back to the station with us so we can trace where this message came from?"

"Yes of course, my shift has ended so that's fine. I will follow you there."

With both Hallie and Fowler on route back to the station and Parker following close behind, Hallie's mind couldn't help but fixate on that message. Which was a good thing in her eyes, the less she thought about her mother and why she was there the better. "What do you think he meant by you have been good so far?"

"Do you think Parker isn't telling us the full story?"

"Wouldn't be the first time, but we will have him at the station with us so can ask him."

Back at the station, all evidence they collected from the hospital was now in a lock up in the station, Hallie received a text message saying forensics had arrived and scanning the 13th floor for prints. Fowler was already in a large oval office with Parker, Gibb, Sergeant, and a few of Gibb's best men to help get a location of the sender of the text message. Hallie sat opposite Parker and looked straight into his eyes. "Parker, something that has been niggling at me since reading that message, when he said you've been good to me so far, what else have you done for him?" The room fell silent, both Fowler and the Sergeant looked over at Hallie. They both knew she was direct, but this was straight to the point.

"I didn't do anything. Well, nothing I thought was bad. He asked me questions about Katie and Alex, asked why I was friends with people who used me. He tried to get in my head and that was when I shut him out. He didn't like that. But was still okay with me. I deal with so many people like it at work so to go home to someone like it was just a big red flag for me."

"Okay, so what did you do to push him so far he just, disappears?" Hallie was digging for some information. "Was it something that you might have said, triggered him maybe to just disappear?"

"Not that I can think of, I mean I felt like I was falling for him. He was a man of mystery. I felt like I could crack him open, but we never where you know… intimate with each other. The more I think of it, think I was just being used." You could see how Parker was disheartened the more he spoke.

"Tell me about him Parker, what was he like, what attracted you to him?" Hallie needed to keep Parker talking just to get a rough idea of his characteristics.

"What wouldn't attract you! Even Katie was shocked the first time she met him, he was a little taller than me, had dark brown hair which was always neatly styled. Usually, short sides and longer top that he would slick back, his build was something you'd see out the movies. I did find it weird that he had no social media, nothing! I mean who now days doesn't have something? Was odd but added to his mystery. He said if he needed someone, he'd always find them. That he did with me! He took to Katie very quickly, like they'd met before, but Katie swore they hadn't. Alex, well Alex didn't like him at all!"

"Why, what makes you say that?"

"He got on with his girlfriend better than he did with Alex. Alex was a jealous type and very protective. One time us three were at a bar down in the town and someone tried hitting on Katie, touched her leg well, Alex ended up breaking his nose and dislocating the matey's wrist."

"Sorry to interrupt but we have a location, I'll bring it up now." Gibb was attaching his findings to the TV screen which was located on a street in a built-up neighbourhood.

"Fuck off!" Parker rose out of his seat and his eyes fixated on the TV screen; he looked like he'd seen a ghost.

"I'm sorry?" Fowler looked over shocked at his sudden outburst.

"That pinpoint, are you sure?" Looking straight over to Gibb ignoring Fowler's question.

"I'm positive, why?" Gibb was never usually wrong, and a simple track of an address was usually quite easy for him to complete.

"Parker, use your words, what is it?" Hallie stood up and moved next to him to try and get him to talk.

"That's, my fucking house. Is he in my house?"

20

Arriving at Parker's house, the police did a check around the inside, outside and surrounding areas for Nathan but all was clear. He had left his burner phone on the step on Parker's front door. Hallie put her gloves on and placed the phone in an evidence bag to see whether they could get any fingerprints off it or if the phone was used to contact anyone else. The phone was still on, that's how they were able to get to a location so quickly, a little black Nokia 215 and Parker was correct, only text and calling for this phone not even a camera on it.

"Okay, all is clear, we are running footage from CCTV cameras from this area and around a perimeter see if we can pick up this man."

"Thank you Simon, keep us posted if your team pick anything up from the cameras."

"Of course, do you want me to take the phone and get Gibb's to run it through?"

"Ah if you could that'll be great thank you." Hallie handed over the sealed evidence bag with the contents of the phone in it to Simon. Simon was part of the crime investigation team here at the constabulary, his well-groomed beard and slick back hair made him look like he should be a male model rather than an investigator but nevertheless he was good at his job and that's all that mattered.

Hallie headed back to the car where Fowler was sitting outside on the pavement with Parker chatting away. "Right Parker, we have an all clear on the building and your apartment so you're free to head back as I know it is late. We will be having you under surveillance and you will have police outside here and at your work also for your protection. It seems like this Nathan is fond of you, so your safety is our top priority here." Hallie seemed genuine but did hope that Nathan would come back to see Parker so they could catch him.

"Yes, thank you. Why do I seem to only find friendship in people that are fucking weird?" Parker began to walk to his front door and entered the building. Police would be outside 24/7 to make sure no one got in or out that looked like Nathan. But deep down, Hallie knew Nathan would come back and see Parker, but she hoped they would catch him before he got there.

Heading back to the station, Fowler began discussing his conversation with Parker to Hallie. "I mean it was nothing too concerning the things he was coming out with, but he mentioned about how patients would vanish like there was a secret hiding spot then re appear like they were there the whole time. I mean I think the place is haunted more than anything?"

"I find it odd how we have visited that hospital a fair few times now and not once has an owner or someone with high authority come to visit us or ask questions, don't you?" Hallie looked over to see Fowler's confusion and agreed how it was odd no one had seen them. They picked up a McDonald's on route back and stayed at Fowler's that night. It made sense as they both were now seeing each other why not just stay together.

6:30 am approached quickly and instead of an alarm going off to wake both Hallie and Fowler up it was a phone call. Hallie answered still half asleep however that soon changed when she sat bolt upright and ended the call which made Fowler wake up and begin to wonder.

"What's happened?"

"We need to go now; Parker didn't show up for his shift this morning. They went to check the building, make sure all was okay and he's dead." Hallie was already getting dressed whilst informing Fowler of the news.

Arriving outside the block of flats which Parker lived in, it had already been cornered off by police. Parker lived on the top floor which was only shared with another tenant on that floor, every other floor had four apartments in. Hallie went under the tape line and headed into the building taking the steps two at a time to get up them faster, Fowler close behind her. As they approached Parkers door Hallie showed her badge to the constable on the door and she entered whilst putting her gloves on. However, it came as a shock to both Hallie and Fowler what had happened. They had never seen anything like this before, and both have seen some messed-up things in their career. "What the-." Fowler couldn't even finish the sentence. He began to look around the room whilst Hallie slowly approached Parker's body.

Forensics were photographing everything they could, it looked like Parker had put up a good fight but the way it ended was not good. Parkers apartment was small but perfect for one person. As soon as you walk in the front door you are in the lounge with an open plan kitchen/dining area. Heading towards the left is a bathroom and the right has one large bedroom and a small room which Parker used as a dress room. However, as you walk straight in the front door this time you have Parker's dead body hung on the wall, what looked like hooks through his collarbones attached to the wall and his back had been sliced open and the skin also nailed to the wall, all of Parker's internal organs were out of his body, everything there except one of his lungs which was very odd. A note had been left written on the large mirror which hung between the kitchen and lounge.

'Sorry it had to end this way my butterfly. But I couldn't trust him anymore or see you alone so better off dead in my eyes.'

"This person is sick, fucking sick!" Fowler added whilst reading the note, he wasn't wrong whoever this is hasn't killed someone like this before. Every killing the victim was drugged. Why Parker, why was he left like this and why like a butterfly?"

"You're not wrong there. What I want to know is how the killer got in when Parker was under protection?" Looking over to PC Kimber and PC Oakly to which both where startled to hear their names.

"Ma'am we had surveillance on the front of the building all evening, nobody entered or left the building all night." PC Kimber spoke on behalf of them both as PC Oakly looked a little bit pale from seeing the body.

"Is there any other access to the building?"

"No ma'am just that door, no fire escape nothing we made sure of it."

"So, the killer must've already been in the building when we came through before putting anyone on the door and-."

"And when they came to check why Parker hadn't left for work and told everyone to evacuate the killer could've slipped out easy."

"Shit!" Hallie began to walk out of the room and walk down the stairs. Fowler spoke with forensics to make sure anything important was sent straight to him or Hallie and began to catch up with Hallie.

"How, how is this piece of shit one step ahead of us every time!" Hallie was angry, but she knew deep down this was just a game to the killer and games are meant to be played and won, she just needed to win. As Hallie looked around the street, people were beginning to gather around, rumours appearing and not one person knowing the extent of what had happened. Before you know it, journalists arrived and getting this on for Breaking news and it is a weekday, so news begins around 6am anyways. Hallie went back inside and knew she needed to concentrate, see if she could notice anything out of the ordinary or odd as she was in Parkers apartment before the murder. That was when she went back to his body and looked closer. Parker's back had been sliced open so neatly, no jagged lines, no botch job, doesn't look rushed, this was neatly done and whoever did it took all the time they wanted to do it.

"Detectives, think this is the most I've seen you both in such short amount of time." Jameson arrived ready to take over and get some answers, which to Hallie's relief was a good sign as he knew everything on this case.

"Indeed it is, shame on the circumstances." Fowler appeared from the kitchen area and began to head over to the body when he noticed something on the wall in the hallway.

"What you seen?" Hallie walked over to the photo, and it was of a butterfly, but just single photo not even framed stuck the wall. Hallie took a photo and then took it off the wall, turned the photo over to and had a false nail stuck to the back.

"Well, I don't think this is Parkers, Jameson can you take this and run any test on it see how old or if it's a false nail or real?"

"Sure can, huh?" Jameson looked closely at the nail and peeled it off the photo to look underneath.

"Huh what?" Fowler asked in confusion as was just a nail but there must be a meaning to this.

"No, nothing well something, I was on a date last night and these were the exact nails my date was wearing. French tip but each nail had a gem on it, I noticed it as her hands where... well somewhere." Jameson looked up and saw both Hallie and Fowler's face with a smirk yet still confused. "Okay so could be a false nail and your date must wear the same?" Hallie wanted the subject to change away from Jameson's eventful night.

"Well, I thought that when I asked her, she said nope all natural, even stated how she had nothing fake, nails, lashes, hair nothing. I mean, attractive right?" Jameson was chuffed with how his night went but then something clicked. If that is her natural nail, that means this could be hers. And why was her nail stuck on the back of butterfly photo in a crime scene?

"Jameson, need you to focus now, did she stay with you for the night or leave?" Hallie knew time was ticking, this must be another game.

"No, we done... stuff in the car, I took her home as she said she had work early and no way of getting there if she stayed."

"What time?"

"I got home around 1am so reckon dropped her back around 12.12:30 ish. You don't think this is hers, do you?" Jameson began to look concerned, which was a first as he was the one known as the sarcastic and charming one, but you could see the panic begin to rise in his face.

"I hope not but I am not ruling anything out, what is her name and what does she look like? We need an address also to see if she is still there. Are all her nails on and where she gets them done as could be a common trend look now." Hallie wrote down all the information she needed, got a name, address and ran a quick background check on her.

Miss Daisy Green, 31-year-old resident doctor at Southampton General Hospital. Specializing in Neurological Surgery, no partner, children emigrated from Seattle USA for a surgical program which involved some of the best surgeons around the country. Her residency she was staying at informed officers who went to check out the scene that she hadn't been home yet assuming she stayed out with someone. Red flag number one.

Contacting the hospital to see whether she may already be at work, not arrived at the hospital. The hospital's IT department checked to see if her key card had been used at all and the last time it was used was yesterday evening around 7:30pm. Red flag number two.

Hallie and Fowler were on route back to the station when Hallie rung Jameson and put the call straight on speaker.

"Jameson, when did you meet Daisy?"

"Last night, in Fusion Bar. Told me about what she did for a living, as did I, we had drunk together and well slept together in my car why?"

"What time?"

"I got to the bar around 6 and she approached me pretty quickly as was still on my first beer."

"Okay, will call if need anything. Oh, did you get her number, a photo or even her socials?"

"Nope nothing, she said she knew where to find me if she needed me, she had a shitty little phone on her though I thought was just something the hospital gives their staff if they on call and need to go in for an urgent call maybe?"

"Nokia?" Fowler questioned already knowing the answer.

"Yeah, little black one."

Hallie ended the call and arrived back at the station they both headed to their office to gather any evidence and get the team briefed on what has happened so far and next steps. Hallie didn't enjoy playing leader, but she needed more eyes and bodies on this case as whoever the killer is good, and from what it sounds like they have help.

21

Board room, the largest room in the constabulary and for good reasons. Reasons like this one. The room was a large oval shape, a neutral look, dark brown walls which went only halfway up to the wall and the rest was an off-white colour, all tables and chairs laid out in rows and three large TVs hung on the wall which all the chairs faced. Detectives, IT, Forensics, and some PCs began to take their seats and the room slowly filled. The sergeant was on a tall chair on the front right-hand side of the room speaking with two other detectives. The room was now full, and everyone was either in their seats or stood talking to others. Hallie and Fowler entered the room and silence broke; you could hear a pin drop. Everyone took their seats, some with note pads and a pen, some taking the information they are yet to receive by just listening. Hallie plugged in a USB drive to the back TV and took the wireless clicker remote to be able to move the slides and point the laser pen to relevant parts. Hallie had a large dislike for meetings, especially if she was the host of one, but time to put her personal feelings aside and brief everyone.

"Right, think everyone in this room knows why they are here, and I know Sergeant has briefed you all slightly but here is a reminder, just in case." Hallie kept a calm tone but was straight to the point with everything she said. "Everything you hear today stays between us, no talking to other departments, no asking others for insight, no mention to no one. We are going to be working as a team on this and the less the outside knows the better. Warning for anyone who is sensitive to

I'd Kill For You

blood, dead bodies and any evidence shown in following slides please excuse yourself now as this case is not for the faint hearted." Hallie stopped talking to allow anyone to leave the room if they felt it necessary to do so. No one left, just people looking around at each other. "Great, let's get into it."

"As you all know, previous killer nicknamed Night Stalker was arrested and sentenced to life in prison. He then died 6 months into his sentence from suicide. Now, that same killer is the one committing these murders. The wrong person was convicted, and we have reasons as to why, but we will get to that." Hallie clicks to the first slide which is Katie Wilson's dead body, a few people look away but look back to show they are here to stay.

"Katie Wilson, daughter of Judge Wilson who many of us know was found dead in the park, all belongings still with her and last known where abouts was with her boyfriend. Katie was stabbed seven times however this was not cause of death as she was drugged before hands."

Hallie clicks onto the next slide which is of Alex's body to which Fowler stands up and begins to talk. "Alex Jonoski, boyfriend of Katie Wilson. Also drugged but was barely alive when found, died shortly after being given CPR. This bottle labelled 'drink me' was left next to the victim. The way we found Alex was that there were co-ordinates left by the killer on Katie's laptop." Now for the next slide which made nearly everyone in the room turn their heads and make a slight discomforting sound, which was valid.

Hallie began, "Dr Parker Fields, our third victim was found in his apartment like this. We had Parker in the station that evening questioning him as he had received a message from our top suspect which pinpointed the suspect at Parker's house. We had left Parker under surveillance but still not enough for the killer to slip past them. Each of these victims were friends with each other and our top suspect is this man. Nathan Smith."

A few gasps left the room as they knew this was the name of the previous killer. But waited to ask questions till the end. Fowler then began with another slide. "We believe that Nathan goes by James Wilson also. Judge Wilson and his wife had another child, an older sibling to Katie, James, who was troubled and was admitted to St Catherine's hospital. We believe that this James Wilson goes by

Nathan Smith as a cover up and tried to take everything the Wilson family loved like they had done to him. But got carried away when Katie's boyfriend suspected something was going on. Nathan/James befriended Parker and made Parker believe he wanted a relationship with him when in fact all he wanted was Parker."

Pens were scribbling down when Hallie and Fowler were giving their orders and what jobs needed doing to help catch this person. The next major thing for them to do was find Daisy as she either was missing or is part of this. At the end of this briefing Hallie offered the chance for anyone to ask questions. When no one took the opportunity too she began to inform them once again that any intel, new information or anything suspicious they might find report to herself or Fowler ASAP.

As everyone left the only people left in the large boardroom were Hallie, Fowler and the Sergeant. "Well, the media have released some insight as to the killings, only the statements I have released which is good. Might scare the killer off slightly or if someone can see something out the ordinary report it. We also have a name and address on that letter you found in the hospital, but you'll have the same response I did as to who it is!" The Sergeant gave a look to Hallie and Fowler expecting a response, but both waited quietly for Sergeant to tell them. "Pauline Deere. Ring any bells?"

"Fuck off, is it?" Both Hallie and Fowler knew this name and that reaction was as shocking as expected.

"Indeed, we have had two officers collecting her and bringing her into the station for questioning, she is in room 5 when you are both ready." The sergeant led the way to the interrogation room and headed for a separate door which enabled him to listen to everything said.

"Mrs. Deere, I'm not sure whether you will remember me or not but I'm…"

"I know who you are dear, I remember you both well. Detective Jones and Detective Fowler, my question is what I can do for you?" Mrs. Deere was an elderly lady who was very well spoken and had a fortune to her name. Her late husband was part of the Deere family who invented the famous machinery John Deere and Company which dated back to 1837. The Deere family always had assets to this as their fortune still grows to this day, however Mrs. Deere lived alone, her only child died, and she was never able to have any more children as her husband passed away when their son was aged 9. Mrs. Deere was still very mobile for her age, she did nothing to stop her slowing down. Her short Grey hair, which was always up, small, rounded glasses which fit her oval face lovely was a key feature.

"I'm glad, that saves the introductions and can go with a how have you been since last we saw each other Mrs. Deere?" Hallie wanted to be polite and the conversation flowing with Mrs. Deere, she was a known talker but the more they could get out of her the better.

"Indeed dear, well not a lot, still the same routine as all those years ago when we last spoke. I assume I am not here for a catch up though Detective, this is about them killings, isn't it?" Mrs. Deere looked up to both Hallie and Fowler, her blue eyes were magnified by her glasses which showed them watery.

"Unfortunately, yes, you see Mrs. Deere we originally thought your son was behind all of this. However, we now have reason to believe he was tricked into believing he had committed those crimes." Hallie didn't want to give Mrs. Deere too much information at once, she wanted to get a feel for her reactions and what she might say.

"I understand, however my son wasn't innocent, I know that even if he didn't commit those crimes, he would still be a part of them."

Fowler sat up in his chair and left his arms on the table in front of Mrs. Deere, opening a beige colour folder where he pulled out some photos. "Mrs. Deere, do you recognize any of these people?"

Mrs. Deere looked over the photos and lent a bit closer, pointing down at Parker's photo, "That is the young nurse who looked after my son, he worked on the same ward he was on. Also remember seeing that girl but she didn't work there when I used to visit, she would help the nurse on occasions."

"Mrs. Deere, how long ago did you used to visit your son? When did you stop and why?"

Mrs. Deere bowed her head, looking disappointed with herself and embarrassed at what she was about to reveal. "I stopped around 5 years ago, my son would just tell me things I didn't need to know, would ask me to find information about others. I was happy to help at first but then one day he snapped, saying I cared only for myself, didn't love him and I wasn't his mum, that hit me hard the thought he was turning against me, so I stopped all visits and let him be. Wasn't too long after that I rang the police on the photos, I saw on the news about the murders happening at the time. I was truly convinced it was him, he would obsess with people so badly that once they were in his head, they stayed there."

"So, we came across this also, could you explain why you sent and wrote this?" Hallie took the photo out of the Wilson's family and handed it to Mrs. Deere; however, Mrs. Deere's reaction was not one they expected. She looked somewhat happy, a small smile appeared across her face, she placed her hand over her heart.

"I gave this to a young boy who I would have happily adopted and taken home with me, James his name was. He was a very kind sweet boy. I had developed a bond with him because my own son would not love me, he did. He would send me happy birthday cards, any time I would visit my son and he wouldn't see me, James would spend time with me, and I truly cared for this boy."

"So, why did you send him a card of the Wilson's family?"

"Because he asked about them, he knew their names and asked if he could find a photo of them so he could hang it up. He had no family to visit him, no one cared, he was such a kind-hearted boy. He explained he was picked on because everyone had photos of their families and he wasn't. I gave him the photo as a present but assured him I would be his family if he wanted one."

"And did he?" Hallie could see that Mrs. Deere was very genuine and wanted love, she had no one.

"He did, but he then just vanished, the staff at St Catherine's wouldn't disclose any information on him as I wasn't direct family or a guardian. To this day, I don't know where or what happened to him." Mrs. Deere looked heartbroken, she did care for this boy and wanted to help him, you could see that but at this rate he is the prime suspect for the killings.

"One final question Mrs. Deere, has James tried to contact you at all or anyone recently?"

"No, only people I speak with are my friends who I meet twice a week for games or tea and cake."

Hallie and Fowler ended the interview and Mrs. Deere was still happy to help any way she could so that is a good sign. Hallie has Mrs.

Deere under surveillance just in case James is with her and she is covering it up out of love.

"Detectives, my office!" The sergeant gave no explanation nor any other words, it was like Hallie and Fowler was back in school and being told off by the teacher. All they both hoped was that their little secret was still a secret, no one would no they was sleeping together, or suspect anything surly?

"Yes sir?" Both detectives are standing in the office whilst the Sergeant is pacing before he finally takes a seat. "Take a seat both of you." They do as they are told, however, both not looking too comfortable as unsure what this is about.

"Does Butterfly mean anything to either of you?" Sergeant lent onto his desk looking at both Hallie and Fowler, neither understanding the question.

"No, don't think so why?" Fowler answered however Hallie stayed quiet, intrigued to know why.

"Because it keeps appearing, the photo in victim's apartment, he was cut open and pined like he had wings, the drug used on both victims is also a chemical used to gas insects so they can be stuffed in a way for decoration, and now this!" Sergeant spun his computer screen around, and a photo of a butterfly appeared, underneath the words *'times ticking'*. The photo was like a boomerang photo which enabled the butterfly's wings to move slightly back and forth, the message was written in fancy script which looked handwritten. Question is, what is the time ticking for, another murder?

22

Arriving back in the office with the new information that the killer has another member of the departments email to contact, with no trace to them. IT are trying to find where the sender is as we speak but at this rate probably will get no luck.

"Butterflies, why a butterfly?" Fowler asked as soon as the door to their office closed behind them. He planted himself in his office chair and began to look over any notes or information they had. "Butterfly, I mean could it be a new thing, something we missed? What you- Hal?" Fowler stopped talking immediately when he saw Hallie's face, tears welling up her eyes, lent up against the door not moving. "Hallie?" Fowler rose and began to walk over to her when she zoned out of her daydream and looked petrified. Fowler didn't move a step closer; he hasn't seen Hallie look this scared since Afghanistan. "Hal, please talk to me?"

"Butterfly..." Hallie still hadn't made eye contact with Fowler but kept her eyes down.

"When Sergeant said does that mean anything to either of us, you didn't answer? What does it mean?" Fowler still hasn't taken a step closer to Hallie, space is what she needed, and this must be something serious.

"My mum, she used to call me Butterfly as a kid. But when I was taken back in Afgan, he called me his little butterfly. The one we could never identify, the one that would happily torture me, he would have never known my mum called me it, but she only did when she wanted something, but he called me it like he... like he owned me." Hallie still not making eye contact, this was a past trauma and a big trauma to say the least. "Before the extraction, before he killed Doctor Hague, we were both separated. He had me tied up and just in my shirt and underwear. Saying how I'm his, and he will take every bit of me, he sliced my back because I didn't 'behave'. Never using my name like the others, he would say 'my butterfly'. It can't be him; it can't fucking be. I have shut him out my head, locked every memory of that time, it can't Adam!" That was it, Hallie couldn't hold back her tears and she slid down the door into a ball and began to cry. Fowler knelt and cradled Hallie, just holding her and attempting to calm her. Hallie was one that could hold her emotions well, but this man tortured her mentally and physically and no one else knew about this. Hallie didn't disclose that to anyone in the army.

"Hal, you are safe, I will make sure no one ever hurts you again okay. I'm here okay, I'm here." Stroking through her hair and holding her tight was the best thing Hallie could have right now. Knowing she would have to tell Sergeant this information was a hard pill to swallow but one that needed to be done.

The Sergeant's reaction was expected, he was shocked. This meant that the killer has now targeted Fowler and Sergeant through email but linked a past trauma of Hallie's in the mix. "So, you mean to tell me that this killer could be the same person who held you hostage when you served in the army Jones?"

"Yes sir. No one knew this I didn't disclose the nickname to my superiors or Fowler, no one knew just myself. It could be just one big coincidence or…"

"Or Detective this killer is targeting you, getting under your skin, I don't know but I know you. So, what's next?" The sergeant took a seat opposite Hallie and Fowler and looked at them both awaiting an answer.

"We go through all evidence again, try find any leads, people who may know them, talk to other doctors or residence at the hospital. Find out how they all link. We need to talk to the Wilson's again make them aware of any updates as well as Alex and Parker's families. We will catch whoever it is." Hallie was back to her old self, focused determined. You wouldn't have thought that she had just had a breakdown.

"Okay so we have a prime suspect, Nathan Smith aka James Wilson. We know he was in the same ward a Mrs. Deere's son so they knew each other, which must mean that they became friendly enough for Nathan/James to convince her son who was the real Nathan Smith he was the killer. Maybe we can find anyone else of sane mind who can help us that was also in same ward as them, previous doctors, patients family members? What you think?" Hallie glanced over to Fowler who was staring at the large board which hung the victims' names and other information on the killings.

"Ye-yeah that's the best plan, maybe speak with the Wilson's again see if anyone random has targeted them. Does Parker have any immediate family?" Fowler finally focused, he grabbed his laptop and began typing to log onto his emails.

"Nope, no one. No parents, he was brought up in central London but no immediate family. Looks like he was adopted so maybe we can track down his adopted parents?" Hallie followed in Fowler's footsteps and began sending an email to a colleague in another department to ask to get any family history on Parker.

"You've got to be fucking kidding me. Is this a joke?" Fowler stood up and began pacing, arms around his head. "I'll kill this fucker when I get my hands on him, I swear!"

"What are you talking about?" Hallie is concerned began to rise and she went to look on Fowler's laptop when she saw the reason for his behaviour.

'Detective Adam Fowler, I thought I'd contact you again seeing as I already have you in my contacts. How are you enjoying your little hunt for me? I warned you it would be hard, but I insist on giving you help as you have what I want. You have it all and I dislike you for that very much. But you are not the one I want. All will be revealed soon enough, enjoy my little butterfly, we will meet soon enough.'

The email had a small black butterfly attached to the bottom of the message which, like the previous one sent to the sergeant moved. No words, Hallie stood up walked straight to her desk and called Gibb to get up to their office and track where the email came from. Next was to get the Sergeant to the office but there was no answer to his phone, so a simple text was sent to him, so he is warned. Finally, over to Fowler to figure out what is going on in his head.

"It is a mind game okay, he's playing us, we haven't found him yet, so he is just trying to get in our heads okay." Hallie's attempt to calm Fowler was a slight success but not enough.

"Why the fuck is this sick bastard emailing me and what could I possibly have that he wants? My job, my house, my family, my sane fucking mind? My…" Fowler paused and looked back at the email, quickly read it over again and looked up to Hallie. "Fuck."

23

10 years ago

Hallie laid on the cold cement floor, shaking not only from the cold but from the beating she had just received for not giving in to these people who was kidnapping her and Doctor Ashira Hague. Both were left in the room alone, men stood outside to make sure who went in was working with them, and both Hallie and Ashira didn't get out. "Corporal Jones, what did they do to you, here." Ashira crawled over to Hallie which made Hallie come to her senses and go into survival mode, to show no signs of weakness and to make sure they both get out alive.

"Ashira, we have known each other for a while now, and given the current situation we are both in please, call me Hallie." Hallie sat up with a groan, she knew she had broken a rib or something, she'd be shocked if nothing was broken the amount she was kicked.

"Why have they done this to you and not me?" Ashira began to look around the room, confused and scared. Ashira was a petite woman who in her mid-30's and worked as a doctor for the hospital in the army.

"Because they saw my dog tags before I could hide them properly. They know who I work for and want information about my team and what they plan to do, when they will attack. Course I got an extra bit of kicking for being a stubborn cow and giving them a taste of their own medicine." Hallie had a smirk come across her face and a slight chuckle which soon stopped realising the pain it left her in. "They will most likely do the same to you Ashira just for being with me. They think you work at the hospital so I believe they will want you alive so you can help any of their own soldiers if they get injured."

"I'll make sure they never walk again if they expect me to help them!" Ashira was a strong lady who had seen her fair share of traumas but never being taken herself. "Hallie, you could've gotten away, you should have left me."

"Yeah, well that is not me, I leave no one behind. My team will find us and get us out of here I don't doubt that in any way."

The next day, Hallie and Ashira were only given minimal food to survive with and small amounts of water throughout the day. Afghanistan heat was enough to make anyone thirsty just thinking about it, so this was a struggle and a half for them both. Ashira received her first beating that morning, she did disclose she worked at the hospital but lied and said that she only was with the army because they had a man, they asked to help which was one of Fladhir's men. This meant she only left that room with a black eye, and bruised wrists from the rope being so tight which held her up while throughout the interrogation. When she was flung back in the same room as Hallie, they wasted no time in grabbing Hallie and taking her to be interrogated once again. This time stood a very tall well-built man who wore a black hood and kept his face covered. All you could see was his dark brown eyes, everything else was covered, this made Hallie wonder who and why he was here. He was not from around here.

"Round two is it, had to bring in your Pitbull to help is that the case." Hallie knew this would piss them off, but she didn't care, she knew she wouldn't say anything they would have to kill her. "What's up Fladhir, can you and your men not handle not getting your own way you send some random son of a bitch in who looks the part to try and scare me?"

"My dear, no, he will just torture you till you talk. His own request though, he seems to have taken a special liking to you. Will leave you to it then." Fladhir nodded to the hooded man who nodded back, and he looked over to his men who followed him out. You could hear the old lock turn when they locked the door behind them.

"Okay, so what are you on mute or something?" Hallie was tied up, arms together but pulled up to the ceiling, her legs just about touching the floor. She was vulnerable but their mistake for leaving her legs untied.

"I am not mute, just enjoy the quiet sometimes, like the unknown." The hooded man spoke dragging an old white plastic chair and sat right in front of her. He had an American accent which was the first thing Hallie noticed.

"American hey, bit out your way isn't it being here?"

"Oh, I know, but you're here so that's a bonus itself. Hmm, don't like how they tied you, easy access to get away with, lets adjust that." Now Hallie had her arms apart like a wingspan but still legs left untouched.

"What do you want with me?" Hallie's tone still had not changed, she was stern and made sure she didn't show any emotion.

"I wanted information, I will still get information. But the more I look at you the more I think to myself how someone as gorgeous as you would be doing something like this."

"Could say the same for you but you gone for the typical stalker look, you know black hoodie, black jeans, timberland boots and a hood, but topped it off with the black balaclava round your face, very original!" Hallie's sarcasm usually was too much but what does she have to lose.

"Even your voice, very nice. You'll be mine now Butterfly." The hooded man stood up and whispered this in Hallie's ear, he had a deep voice, but this was not a nice thing.

"I am no one's!" Hallie nudged him off and tried to get any other features from him.

"Now now, no need for that, just give me what they want to know then we can leave."

"We! Absolutely fucking not. Do you really think I would leave with you?" Hallie's voice was beginning to rise.

"Fine, hate to hurt my beautiful butterfly but guess you'll have to learn the hard way." With that a hard punch went straight into Hallie's stomach, instantly feeling sick but knowing she could get through this.

"Oh, I knew I'd like you, you wanna put up a fight. Too bad." With that another hard punch to the side of her rib cage, still attempting not to make a sound but inside she was screaming. Another hard hit again and then Hallie fell to the floor, he had untied the rope. Thinking now would be the perfect time to run, Hallie attempted it get to the door, but the hooded man grabbed her. Hallie was kicking, hitting, doing anything to get out of his grip but he was too much, too strong. He pinned Hallie down to the floor kneeling on both her arms and sitting on her waist so she couldn't move, all Hallie could do was see him. See those dark eyes, not a speck of happiness in them.

"I don't want to hurt you butterfly, but I will." With that, his large hands were stroking through Hallie's hair and grazed down her face which ended up around her neck. His grasp is getting tighter, and tighter. Still, no words leaving Hallie's mouth just gasping for air, she then saw everything start to go fuzzy. This was it; she was being strangled to death until he let go. Hallie began to get any air she could into her lungs to get her full sight back. With whatever broken bones she has she coming to accept this is going to be harder than she thought.

"Like I said, I'm not going to kill you. Well not yet anyways." The hooded man carried Hallie back to the room where Ashira was kept, and he chucked her to the floor. Ashira was unconscious and Hallie knew what they would endure next, was not going to be fun.

24

Hallie already knew what Fowler meant. She knew it when she first read the email, she had hoped he wouldn't pick up on it, but he did. Hallie looked him dead in the eye and waited for his next words. Any words, because she had none, nothing to say.

"Hallie, he knows." Fowler was still in the same position, not moved a muscle. "He knows about us; I have what he wants."

"Yes, seems that way." Hallie is now coming to terms with what could be at stake here. Fowler has a family, he has a lot of things, you name it, he has it. But Hallie on the other hand has no one, just Fowler. If something was to happen to him, well who knows what she would do. But the killer doesn't work that way, he plays games.

"Adam, we need to get your family under surveillance, safe house just get them away!" Hallie began to call the team who deal with 24-hour watches.

"They already are Hal,"

"What, how?"

"They were put in protection when I got the first email as a precaution and will remain there till the case is closed. I don't know where abouts which is a good thing as if I went to go see them, could be followed then, well who knows."

"And you failed to let me know this was done?" Hallie's tone now very strong, her eyes looked betrayed but grateful it was done already.

"No one knows, I only knew because I used to call them daily now, I am unable to. Just, was easier to keep quiet. But that isn't the problem right now is it and you know it." Fowler and Hallie never argued but both their voices began to rise.

"Oh, I'm sorry. Okay that's what you want. I'm sorry I was taken hostage 10 years ago, I'm sorry the person who beat me till I lay there wondering if I was going to die is still after me, I'm sorry I got this job and you have me as a partner, I'm sorry it has taken all these years for us to fall for each other. What do you want me to say Adam. Okay, this is as new to me as it is to you. I don't know how long this psycho has been watching me and why he killed them people. Fuck I don't even know what he looked like when he beat me so hard, I could feel the blood dripping down my face, the bruises already appearing. I'm sorry I didn't mention the nickname before, but it was something that I locked away and wanted to leave my mind forever okay. So yes, you want to hear it I am scared, you want to hear that I am terrified that he will do what he did to me all those years ago, well there you have it Adam. Not so tough am I, no because the both of us had it drilled into our heads at a young age to hide emotion, so I do." Fowler was speechless, he didn't mean to hurt Hallie, but maybe that was something that needed to come out. He moved his chair out of the way and grabbed Hallie, held her to his chest, both arms wrapped around her. Hallie released a deep breath, a sigh of relief.

"I would never hurt you okay, you are the strongest person I know who has been through hell and back. Yes, I was annoyed you didn't tell me all those years ago about the nickname, but it doesn't matter now. Okay, you are safe, and that prick is going nowhere near you. Do you understand me, I'll kill him before he ever lays a finger on you again. You are coming to live with me." Hallie's head lifted off Fowler's chest, looked him dead in the eyes to see if he meant that.

"What do you mean, live with you?" Hallie stuttered; she had never lived with anyone before. But if they got caught, they were screwed.

"You heard me, I would have had you move in the day we came back from base. I have always loved you Hal, but I need you under my roof, so I know you'll be safe. Okay?" This didn't seem like a question, more a demand but Hallie was okay with this. They spent so many nights together anyway so wouldn't be anything new.

"Okay."

Three sharp knocks arrive on the door and the hug they both were in soon separated, Hallie wiping her face and Fowler answering the office door. "Sorry, would've been quicker if they didn't have a million-tech people on site wanting my help. Right let's find out where this little devil is." Gibb arrived with his laptop and a rucksack full of wires. This enabled him to plug Fowler's computer into his laptop and begin coding to find where the sender of this email was.

"I'll be back in a minute; I'll go brief Sergeant."

Hallie left the room before Fowler could ask if she wanted him to come. Arriving at the Sergeant's office she entered and explained the email.

"So, Jones you are telling me that this killer is now targeting my staff?"

"Not exactly, I don't believe the killer is wanting us dead, I believe it is a threat and the killer is just enjoying his little game too much. We have Gibb in our office right now coding the email to see where it was sent and hopefully, we will have something."

"I need to take this call but keep me in the loop."

Hallie grabbed three cups of coffee and headed back to the office. So many thoughts were going through her mind, what if's and how can it be. But by the time Hallie came out of her daydream she was already at the office door.

"So it was in the building, again?"

"Seems that way, or that the person who sent it hacks our server and can change his location which would take a very smart person to do. I mean I can do it but took me years to master." Gibb and Fowler are already in conversation which from what Hallie has already heard is a dead end again.

"Okay so now what?" Fowler looks over smiling to Hallie and a thank you for the coffee.

"We don't use emails, you don't use that laptop, we give you a whole new person, someone he would've never heard of. Gibb can keep your laptop, run any test he can on it to find out if can get a pinpoint and we go from there."

"Leave this with me, I have sent you all the data from the old phones and USB stick, so you have all the information. I know what you both are like when it comes to working late." Gibb smirked and left the office with Fowler's laptop.

Just as Hallie was about to continue her phone rang.

"They have Parker's adoptive family records being sent over to me now. Let's see, okay so this explains how he afforded medical school."

"Why do you say that?"

"Because his adoptive parents were Lord and Lady Laing, from Cheltenham London. Both wealthy people but had Parker as their only child."

"Perfect let's go speak with them." Fowler began to get up and get his coat when he soon looked on Hallie's laptop screen to see why she hadn't gotten up to go as well.

"Bugger"

"Yep, died 5 years ago in a helicopter accident. So, Parker must've invested in inheritance and gotten himself through medical school. That's why he had no lease on his apartment, everything was bought outright and in his name."

"Right well it is getting late so let's go back to mine have something to eat and get out of this office. We can go talk to the Wilson's tomorrow and go through the evidence from the last cases too. After today think we need some space from the office, don't you?" Fowler grabbed his keys and began to leave, Hallie close behind him.

As they drove Hallie knew all the turns and stops to get from the station to Fowler's. Realising he had now missed two turns she began to question where she was going.

"Where are you taking me?"

"Back to your house, you're packing all the clothes and bits you need and getting them in my house. Can't risk leaving you alone, besides I meant what I said earlier." Fowler helped Hallie get any clothes and bits she needed from her place and loaded it all in the boot and back seats of his car. Feeling somewhat happy yet nervous, what if he hates living with her, what if spending all this time together will make him hate her. What ifs. Hallie kept quiet; she knew her mind could be a burden so it was easier to keep her thoughts to herself, so she didn't ruin the happiest moment she had in a long time.

25

Finally finishing unloading the car with all of Hallie's clothes and personal bits they were ready to eat which was fortunate as Fowler had ordered food in. Both planted themselves on Fowler's large grey sofa, eating away and a sitcom program playing in the background. "Well, could most definitely get used to this." Fowler grabbed both of Hallie's legs and placed them over his legs.

"I could too, must admit it is nice that we don't have to keep going back and forth now." "Let's just hope you don't get sick and tired of me." Hallie chuckled.

"I would never, if I did think you would've seen me gone a long time ago." Fowler looking over at Hallie, he grabs hold of her and pulls her close. It isn't very late but both being so exhausted mentally and physically an early night was a good idea.

"Hal, I know that you probably don't want to talk about it, but I have to ask."

"Okay?"

"This person that gave you the nickname, do you remember anything about him? What he looked like?" You knew Fowler was hesitant asking this, but this must have been playing on his mind for some time.

"He had an American accent; was tall I would say around 6ft 4 maybe taller but was completely covered. He wore a black hoodie, balaclava, jeans, and boots which were steal toe caps, I remember them. All I saw was his eyes, they were a dark brown, nearly black I would say. Why you ask?"

"Because I just thought if you knew or recognized anything about him maybe we could find him. But Parker didn't mention about him having an American accent, did he?"

"No, but he could've faked an accent. Faked everything to get close to the people he targeted. I just don't understand why them?" Both Hallie and Fowler were led in bed arms around each other. Fowler knew this was a hard subject for Hallie, but he had to know.

The next morning was bliss, both Hallie and Fowler had a fresh mindset and began going through the evidence before heading out to ask questions of a few people in relations to the victims. Before they leave the office Gibb storms through the wooden door, he looks like he has been running here or looks like he has had the scare of a lifetime by a ghost of some sort.

"Gibb, you look, well sweaty?" Hallie was looking Gibb up and down wondering what got him in this state. It was 9am and he was in different clothes so he must have gone home, but looking at him he might need to go back home for a shower.

"The email, it came from the station again." Gibb breathlessly said.

"Okay, so same as last time, something else must be going on for you to be looking like that?"

"Yes well, I tracked it and tried to find where the email was sent, and it was from Sergeant's office!"

Fowler chocked on his morning coffee, "Sergeant's, are you sure?"

"Positive, I am waiting for him to get in so can get on his computer see if it was sent from the computer itself or hacked and made to look like was from it. I will call when have an update for you both." Gibb left the room and headed over to Sergeant's office, Hallie knew that they both would be wasting time if they stuck around, Gibb would call if anything they needed to know.

"Right well think we need to start at the hospital, maybe meet the person who runs it, can we get some information on who this is?" Fowler was ready to get on his laptop to find out the information he needed, but he still hasn't received his replacement laptop. As he went to sit down at his desk, Hallie just started to laugh because it looked so empty without anything on it.

"Piss off, I forgot okay."

"I can tell." Hallie still chuckling, she has the name of who they need to see, and they head back to St Catherine's.

Upon arrival however today was not like any before. There were many vans which labelled 'Patient Transport' and people coming out of the hospital. It looked as if it was being evacuated for some reason. Hallie and Fowler approached the front doors, moving around people, this was the busiest and most chaotic they had seen this place. There was a tall man, very slim build at the desk. As they approached him, he looked over his glasses, looked up and down at both Hallie and Fowler and attempted a guess as to why they would be there. "Are you here to collect a patient? Or here about something else?" The tall man looked as if he had no fat or muscle to his body, just skin. He had dulled grey eyes and looked as if he had just been brought back from the dead. Hallie looked at his lanyard which hung loosely around his neck and stated the name Dr Kalvin Drudge.

"Well, you are just the man we are looking for. Haven't met in person yet, I'm Detective Hallie Jones and this is my partner Detective Adam Fowler. I was informed you would be expecting us as we would like a little chat."

"Ahh, yes detectives I was informed, it has slipped my mind. As you can see, we are too busy for a chat today. We are moving all our patients to other facilities." Dr Drudge looked back down at his clipboard and the back at the computer screen to mark off something.

"I can see that; may I ask why you are moving all the patients away?"

"Because we have been closed down, this building is just too unsafe and the people who own it don't want to pay the money to fix or renovate so we had no choice. For the welfare of my patients, I have been nonstop for months attempting to find new homes for everyone."

"I see, we can see you are very busy Dr Drudge so we won't keep you, just a couple of questions then we will be out of your hair." Hallie looked over at Fowler who had a smirk appear over his case as Dr Drudge is a bald man who looked like his hair had fallen out from stress.

"Of course."

"Firstly, is there any staff members you have that worked around 10/15 years ago maybe longer?"

"Not that work here anymore no, everyone that is here now I think the longest staff member is myself and that is 8 years."

"Secondly would you mind now the building is going to be empty if we have our teams looking around. As you know Dr Fields was murdered and we are trying to get to the bottom of this case so we can catch his and Katie's killer." Dr Drudge gave his full attention when Hallie said this, he had the kind of face that if he was in a horror movie, you'd be the first to run.

"Yes, I worked with them both, so young but so full of potential. We have your warrant which is still in date so please help yourself. All paperwork and contents will be remaining in the building for maximum of 2 days while we sort and get all the relevant parts sent with the patients to their new facilities."

"Thank you. We will be in touch."

Fowler stepped outside to make the call for their team to come to the hospital and inspect it. Hallie headed straight to Parker's office to see if there would be anything there of use. As she entered this seemed to be the only room that had any warmth to it. Beginning with the filling cabinet going through paperwork, nothing of importance as yet. Opening his desks draws just to find some snacks, stationary and note pads all of which had no relevance until the top draw had a lock on it. Which was odd as it is usually the bottom draw. Hallie managed to get it open, using brute force which triggered Fowler to come charging in thinking something had happened.

"Did you really need to break the desk?"

"Yes, the draw was locked, and I wanted to know what was inside of it."

"Couldn't have waited 10 minutes for the team to arrive, they could've picked the lock."

"Nope couldn't wait." Hallie didn't make eye contact as she was filtering through the papers that were found in this draw. Reading through them was information which dated back to the early 2000's. There were circles around random works on each page, Hallie put this into an evidence folder to take back to the station. Another puzzle that needed solving but at least they found something.

Arriving back at the station, Hallie gets straight into the paperwork she found in Parker's locked draw. She began to lay all the sheets of paper in chronological order, it looks like a diary, but not Parker's as his writing was messy. This writing was elegant like calligraphy, written in a ball point pen but all pages written by them same person. Hallie had them all lined up in front of her and began to read. There was 18 pages in total, front and back, which made her chuckle reminding her of a line from her favourite sitcom TV show.

Reading through all the pages, Hallie was invested in whoever had written this. This was personal, this was deep, but she felt some what a connection with the writer. No possible way for this but she felt something.

"Well?" Fowler asked which startled Hallie, he had arrived with two iced coffees and a croissant each.

"I mean, this must be from a patient, I know it isn't Parker but this person talks about the experience they endured being in this place. It is like hell from what they are describing, like torture. Each page has a word circled, I have written them all out, but it looks like the last page has been torn but look here, it has a red line on the tear line so whoever torn it must've torn the last word."

"So, what are these words? And why have these words been circled?" Fowler asking get crumbs everywhere from his croissant.

"No idea, must mean something, I reckon Parker was not meant to have this hence why it was locked away, it's a shame we don't know who wrote it."

"I'm sure we can find out who, so what's the sentence then?"

"You, will, always, find, me, you, can, run, hide, but, in, the, end, you, will, be, his... That's it. There must be another word."

"Maybe, or it ends with 'you will be his' that could be the end of sentence. So, whoever wrote this maybe was of sane mind and trying to get away? Do you think…" just as Fowler was about to finish his sentence Hallie's phone rung and was the Sergeant.

"Yes sir?"

"Can both yourself and Detective Fowler come to my office please, as soon as you can."

"Yes sir, be right there."

"What's up?"

"Sergeant said please. Like overly nice? Somethings going on, he wants us both in his office."

"Shit, he's never nice, maybe he got some last night."

"Think you should ask him that to his face, would like to see that reaction."

"I don't have a death wish but thanks. One thing I will add, is how good your ass looks in them jeans". Fowler was walking slightly behind Hallie and for that exact reason.

"Enjoying your view, I see" chuckling away to herself, amusing the conversation. Just before they entered Sergeant's office Fowler cut Hallie up and whispered in her ear "I know it looks good now but will look better on my face later." Following that Fowler opened the Sergeant's office door giving Hallie no time to defuse the butterflies flying around her tummy and the blush to fade from her cheeks which amused Fowler. But stepping into the office the smile soon faded.

26

The atmosphere of this room was tense, shock for both Hallie and Fowler when they entered the office, out of anything they could've expected this was not one of them.

"Ahh detectives, I believe you already know who this is."

"It's been a while, nice to see that you both are still working together!"

Both Hallie and Fowler automatically stood at attention, arms behind their backs.

"You can both stand at ease, you know that. Besides your boss is the one in the fancy chair, not me."

"Yes, sir. Must still be a force of habit. It is great to see you, it has been, well a long time." Hallie went over to shake his hand. Captain Brooks was a very highly ranked man in the army and was there for both Hallie and Fowler as they worked special forces.

"What do we owe the pleasure sir, coming over to this side after all those years in the army?" Fowler joked as he shakes Captain Brooks hand, he had a good bond with Brooks especially after their last mission with the army was Hallie's extraction.

"You wish but I make at least triple of what you earn, plus I retire soon so I can finally kick my feet up and relax."

"The day we see you retire will be the day I see a pig fly sir. You have been saying you are going to retire for years now!"

"Well, won't be for another 2 years but will happen. But that is not why I am here. Why don't you both take a seat."

This turned serious very quickly, both Hallie and Fowler had a lot of power and authority in their job here but to have their current boss and their old boss in the same room was slightly daunting.

"Your last mission with us was a tough one, for the both of you. I can't imagine the trauma you both endured. You will be pleased to know that 6 months after that we captured Fladhir and his men. But, Hallie, the man that took a certain liking to you we never caught." A weight sunk down in Hallie's stomach. A moment ago, she had butterflies from a comment and now she has a sickening feeling that this person is linked with the killings.

"Anyways, we took this seriously as was on our radar, and Fladhir finally gave us some information on him."

"What information?" Fowler interrupted wanting to know any information about this sick freak.

"He was an ex-navy seal based in USA, he has extensive training and he has knowledge. Left the Navy from a dismissal for hacking the system. He worked alone and we believe he was a part of the Cyprus mission. That is when he must have taken a liking to you Hallie. From then, he knew he was able to target you with Fladhir."

"Who is he?"

"Name is Sebastian Chandler, still to this day unable to get photo of him, must have removed all photos from the data base, no childhood history. Nothing"

Sergeant lent forward hearing his chair creak as he did this, "We have put out a warrant for his arrest, he is a wanted man, we have the teams going through CCTV data base, if that name is used in a shop for a credit card, anything."

"Has anything been found as yet?" Hallie sat back upright, clearing her throat to show she is not affected by this, which was a lie as this was the man who beat her, broke so many of her bones and left her for dead.

"Not yet but we will find him."

"Yes sir, is there anything else." Hallie seeming off but wanting to get out of that room as soon as she could.

"Hallie, you'll find this son of bitch and when you do give me a call. We can have a proper catch up another time, but for now go do what you both do best!" Captain Brook has a special place for them both, he knew this was a short visit.

"Hal, talk to me."

"What is there to talk about, they have a name, that's good we are a step closer. It all makes sense."

"What makes sense?" Fowler began to question but still noticing Hallie hasn't looked up from the paper she found in Parker's desk.

"He was using the case we had all those years ago to send us on a wild goose chase. He used a previous case to make us question our motives if we convicted the right person. He hacked the system; our faces were on the news from it which must've picked up on his radar and that is why he is back!"

"Hallie!" Fowler had both hands on either one of Hallie's shoulders, which made her look him straight in the eye. "That drawing they made of him, is that him?"

"I don't know, the eyes look the same, but I don't know if that is him. Well, it must be him."

"You are allowed to shed emotion okay, don't bottle up whatever you are feeling right now?"

"I honestly don't know what to feel."

"At least he thinks he is still the unknown, we have one up on him. We will find him, and he will rot in prison for the rest of his life. Okay!"

"Okay, you're right." Hallie wanted to get back to work, distract her from seeing that photo, them eyes.

Beginning to realise that the information they found in St Catherine's was somewhat becoming useful. They have found not only the diary from the mystery person with the hidden message but more information on James Wilson. The team that had been sent into St Catherine's had come back with a file on James. Fowler's task was to figure out when James left the facility or anything he had done which was out of the ordinary. But to Fowler's surprise he found nothing of the sort, he had a great record, enjoyed learning, activities and didn't put a foot wrong. So, what went wrong?

"Hal, I think we need to have a chat to the Wilson's see why they sent him to that place and give them the information he was literally a golden child. Maybe they might have heard from him or seen him somewhere?"

"Yeah, I agree, okay well slight problem with that, they won't be back in the area until tomorrow. They are in London, still under surveillance but for a trial there."

"Okay well we will see them tomorrow, I'm going to go and check with Gibb, I need a fucking laptop."

Hallie laughs as Fowler leaves the room. Still looking through all this evidence something doesn't add up. Why would they get drugged and killed, where did he kill Katie and Alex, and why are these three being targeted?

Fowler charges back in the room with a smile over his face. "Meet Patrica Snelling, admin assistant for the police force".

"I assume that is your new log in for the laptop?"

"You assume correctly, I mean that is a pretty unfortunate name but hey, I don't care I have a laptop so that's the main thing."

Working tirelessly, tying up loose ends Hallie keeps being drawn back to the diary entries she had found in Parker's locked draw. In the end she gathers up some of the evidence and takes it back home. Fowler brings just the laptop as still attempting to input everything onto it. Fowler's house was a nice place to work and made Hallie feel at ease, felt like she finally had a place she was wanted.

27

3am- Thursday- Present day

Hallie woke up from a nightmare, she still has them but not as often. Woken from this she headed straight for the bathroom to grab a drink and splash her face with some water.

Hallie was in a state, sweat dripping from her forehead, why was this happening. It is as if every time she closed her eyes, she can see the murders taking place. Being able to see how these poor victims are being killed, a voice in the background just shouting words Hallie can't quite make out it's like everything is fuzzy. A scream bellows from Hallie which feels more like a cry for help, dropping to the floor in such a pain it's as if she is the next victim. "No, no, why are you doing this?" The vision is becoming more and more clear, what the victims looked like before their deaths it's like it's in order, the first victim, the second, so on. Is this an illusion, a nightmare, is Hallie just sleep deprived, or is it another one of the killer's mind games?

As Hallie pulls herself up the bathroom counter, she looks at herself in the mirror, mascara running down her face from her tears, pale as she has ever looked and just stares at herself for what feels like a lifetime. "Why?" she asks herself with a tremble in her voice. A voice which feels like is all around her,

"Because Hallie now, I have you right where I want you. For you to see everything and the reason behind it"

From this Hallie was confronted by the killer, she began to panic and run but was hit over the head. This wasn't enough to knock her on conscious but to make her fall, she began to crawl through the hallway, panic setting through her body. Then everything went black.

A slam of the door woke Fowler from a deep sleep. He had noticed Hallie was no longer next to him but wondered if he just imagined the door shutting or if Hallie has gone somewhere. Her phone still lay on the nightstand and her clothes still draped over the wooden chair in the corner of the room. Fowler goes to see where she is, calling for her he notices that the bathroom tap is still on. Finding blood on his bathroom floor like someone has just been dragged out. Fowler's heart starts to race, he is now shouting Hallie's name and notices blood drops from the bathroom all the way to the front door, he opens it to find no one there, fresh tyre marks on his gravel drive as his car is the only one that drives on it and makes same track every time. Shouting after Hallie, it sets for Fowler that she has been taken. He goes back in the house and sees a photo of a room filled with butterflies, and a message on the back-

'We will meet again'.

"Shit, fuck!" Fowler still shouting, he realises this is helping no one and runs back upstairs to grab his phone. "Pick up, pick up, pick up!" Fowler putting clothes on there was no answer, so he tries again.

"This better be good Fow-"

"She's gone, he has taken her. He's fucking taken her!"

"What? Who?" Sergeant seemed more awake now on the other line.

"Hallie, the prick has taken Hallie. Right under my fucking nose!"

"Where are you I'm on the way with the team?"

Fowler gives his address to Sergeant and waits for him to arrive. Blue lights reflecting across his driveway which Fowler takes no notice of. He is fixated on this photo. How could he have missed this; how did he sleep through it?

"Okay, well we have the team working on cars seen on this route, it's early hours of the morning so unlikely for many cars to be out, luckily there is a shop down the road from here which has CCTV, so we are getting footage from this. Now my question is why was Jones here as well as her clothes and belongings?

Fowler knew this was coming, he could've tackled this alone, but he knew now Hallie was taken and the history with them both he would kill her. But admitting to his boss that he is sleeping with his partner is never an easy thing to do. Fowler still hasn't stood up and stays sat in his armchair with the photo in his hand.

"Fowler, you're going to have to talk to me, now more than ever. No punishments, no lectures, just we need to find Hallie."

"We have been sleeping with each other for few months now. I have loved her since we were in the army together, took me all this time to finally make a move. But we were going to wait till we close this case to then tell you and figure out what would be next." Still no eye contact with Fowler, still looking at the photo of the butterflies, hoping he would know the meaning of it.

"Okay, well I expected it to happen, the killer has a history with Hallie, I am assuming she opened up more with yourself about this?"

"Yes, he tortured her, he wanted her as his own. I promised her she would be safe with me and that she should never have to worry about being taken again and look, she was taken right under my fucking nose. I fucking promised!" Fowler finally stood up and he was angry, his emotions were taking over. He knew he needed to calm down and figure out what and how to get Hallie back, but he has so much anger right now he didn't care if he pissed anyone off, he was going to kill him for even laying a finger on Hallie.

"Sir, we have a plate that could be the suspects." A young officer comes round the corner but is shocked by Fowler's emotions.

"Right send it out I want all teams on the lookout for this, I want a full trail on every camera where this car went and where it is now. Fowler, get your coat, you're coming with me."

Fowler was so used to being the driver that he was slightly relieved he wasn't behind the wheel right now, Sergeant drove a Black BMW x5 which was a new model, very luxurious but quick. Through the Bluetooth of the car, the young officer who found the plate of the car is directing them both the same route the suspect would've driven with Hallie. Now, it was a matter of time.

28

8am

Hallie's head is pounding, like she has been hit by a truck. Beginning to open her eyes, everything is blurry, it takes a few blinks to try and get her eyes to focus. The floor is cold, with only a blanket on the floor, her hand restrained with handcuffs to a chain which attaches to the floor. Hallie is slowly beginning to realise what is going on. Attempting to stand up, her legs fail her, and she falls straight back down, not giving in she tries again a couple more times till she is able to regain balance. The room is cold, old like no one has been in it for years, Hallie thinks wherever she is it has been abandoned for a long time. There is a metal chair in the corner, just alone, Hallie walks over to it but can't reach the chain tugging her back. Still bleeding from her head, she is still in Fowler's long T-Shirt that she slept in and fluffy socks on. Least she had some clothing on, most nights she sleeps in nothing, so this was handy she decided to wear something last night, not that any of that matters right now. Hallie's mind wondering trying to not allow her to panic but she knows what is in order. She has been taken, again, and by the same person.

"Fuck, where the fuck am I?" Hallie trying to walk around the empty room however only able to go so far as the chain attaching her to the floor gives her a certain perimeter to explore. "Okay, no need to panic, they would know by now I'm missing, they are looking for me. I hope. Why is it alwaysme!" Hallie went to sit back down on the blanket she woke on, her head still pounding, she had a concussion of some sort but determined to stay awake, she tried to slip the cuff on her left hand. Glad that they cuffed her left hand, least she could throw a decent punch with her right. Just as she was close to slipping the cuff, she heard footsteps and the lock begin to turn in the door. Looking at the door closely to see who was coming in, her eyes still trying to focus but everything still came fuzzy every other blink she took. Until she saw him walk through and lock the door behind him, he walked straight over to the metal chair and sat down, taking his hood down so Hallie could see his face. It was him, the same man who tortured her in the army, the same one from the photos, the same eyes.

"Nice to see those beautiful eyes open, had to make sure not to hit you too hard, couldn't have you dead now, could I?" his voice deep, husky like if most woman saw him then heard his voice would coo over it. But Hallie despised it, it was the voice which haunted her nightmares, she has so much hatred and now she hates him even more.

"Shame, think I'd prefer to be dead." Hallie still has her sarcastic personality even in crap situations. One time nearly cost her life, but she didn't care, she's been to hell and back many times, what's one more time.

"No, I couldn't do that now could I. Besides, it's finally nice to talk to you again."

"Nice to put a name to the face, Sebastian. What do you prefer, your full name, Seb or Prick. I reckon I could think of a few more but Prick stands well in my head." Hallie wanted answers but was pissed off to the point she couldn't care less what he thought.

"You can call me anything you like Butterfly. Your mine now!" Seb stood up and dragged his chair closer to Hallie, she would be able to reach him now, grab the chain and wrap it around his throat till he stopped breathing. Hallie had to think carefully when to make her move, this was not the right time as she was still bleeding from the head and got dizzy moving too quickly.

"You can stop calling me that!"

"You are my little butterfly, wounded but always able to fly. You're a fighter that's why I like you."

"You are a fucking creep. What you do, stalk me back here, come up with this big plan to kill people to get my attention and then take me?"

Hallie needed his thought process on why he killed those people and if he was the original killer all those years ago.

"Well, seeing as we are going to be spending a lot of time together Butterfly, I will tell you my masterplan. But I do need to clean you up and get some stitches in your head. Least I can do!" Seb seemed genuine but still had an evil to his look. Hallie wasn't fooled.

"Least you can do!! You fucking did this to me, you kidnapped me, don't act the nice guy you are fucking evil. They will find me, and you will rot in prison, Prick!" Hallie stayed strong but knew she needed help, but no help from him.

"Let me just sort this out, I didn't want to hurt you, but you put up a fight. I was just going to drug you in your sleep, and you'd wake up here right as rain."

"Oh, well that makes me feel so much fucking better!" Hallie began to think is this guy for real, is he trying to make her feel better.

"You fought well, I wasn't expecting you to wake up in the middle of the night. But I have you now, that's what matters. If you won't let me touch you let me get a doctor who will stitch it, will you let that happen?" Seb seemed to really feel guilty for hurting Hallie and wanted to fix it.

"Can you uncuff me?"

"Not until you have calmed down and got stitches in."

"Fine, can stitch it. But if you touch me, I will fucking hurt you." Hallie had rage in her eyes. She was confused by the situation, the last time he tortured her but now he wanted to take care of her. Maybe this was another act, or maybe he is just mentally ill. Hallie knows what one she is choosing.

A small older man walked into the room about an hour after Hallie and Seb's conversation, Hallie agreed to get stitches in her head as it was still bleeding from being knocked out. She didn't know how long she had been knocked out for, could've been hours, could've been days, these were questions she needed to ask. The doctor looked around mid 50's, had a kind smile and looked like he wasn't being held here by his own will. He looked like he had just walked in from the outside world. Hallie had no idea.

"Hello, I'm Dr Pearce. Hallie, I know this is a scary situation, but I am no part of it. Seb called as you need some stitches and that is all I am here to do. Okay?" His kind voice gave Hallie some ease.

"Okay."

"Okay, right I'm going to clean it up first, then numb it before stitching it up. It is a pretty nasty gash. I know he didn't mean to hurt you."

"Oh, that make me feel so much better, didn't mean to knock me out and kidnap me?" Hallie still giving sarcastic answers, how could they be serious. How could any of this feel normal, or they think that she would be okay with it. Fruit loops the both of them.

Hallie was now all stitched up and given some food, drink, and pain medication to help with the pain of it. The doctor gave her another blanket before he left. He seemed nice but still no one Hallie could trust. Standing up she got instant head rush but pushed through it. Hallie wanted to find anything she could to help her figure out what was going on and where she was. Looking around the room she notices in the top left corner where the metal chair once was, she sees a camera with a little red light on. That means the camera is on and she is being watched. Seb's first mistake, leaving the chair in Hallie's distance. Hallie grabbed the chair and launched it at the camera causing it to smash to the ground and no more red light, no more being watched. Footsteps came from the distance and instantly she knew she was going to be in trouble for that.

29

Arriving at the old Butterfly Manor, Fowler and Sergeant with a few others of the team begin to fan out and search the perimeter. They had tracked the car that had taken Hallie to this location. The manor was from the early 1900's and was owned by a wealthy family who died in the building from a fire. It has been abandoned now for over 30 year but as real potential to be a beautiful location. Fowler has run through every room he could even through the old rubble which had fallen from the fire. Only half the building was still in tack the rest fallen.

"No sign of her sir." An officer came over to Fowler and Sergeant when they had stopped outside just staring at the boot of the car. It had blood in it which meant she was probably still injured, not too much blood which could cause death but enough there.

"He has left the car here, switched cars and taken her elsewhere, can we get footage from any cameras, least that's one step." Sergeant thinking allowed and Fowler still built with fury, he walks off and goes back in the manor for another check. Nothing there, but he notices something shining from the apple tree around the back, heading over to it is another butterfly photo with another message.

"Sarge!" Fowler shouts but carefully takes the photo off the tree, he turns the photo over to read the message.

'It hurts, doesn't it. Having something or someone you love taken right under your nose. Shame, at least she can put up a fight. Look out for my clues, it's time to play a game Adam. One game you best hope you will be good at. She is a true beauty, would be a shame to see her damaged, again.'

Sergeant reads the message at the same speed as Fowler, he instantly looks up to Fowler and sees his rage building. Fowler was ready for a fight and Hallie was one person he loves more than anyone in the world.

"If he lays a finger on her I will kill him."

"We need to find him first Fowler. And you and I need to go back to the station, get all evidence you both have, get the team together for a emergency meeting. We need all hands-on deck for this if we have any chance of finding her. You need to get a level head back on Adam. I know you care for her but get professional, think, and don't go off on a rampage. You are a defective not in the army, not on special services anymore. You are here and you have the knowledge and ability to find her. She is a fighter and won't give in. We will find her, but you need to focus. Okay?" Sergeant has a point. Since her disappearance, Fowler had been on a rampage, his rage took over, he needs to think and go through what him and Hallie both had found.

Arriving back at the station, Fowler looked like shit, he was on his third coffee of the morning, and it was only 11am. He followed Sergeant to the board room where Hallie and Fowler held the meeting to a large number of members of the force, the same members back in the room with a few other members of the police which had higher rankings than his Sergeant.

"Thank you all for coming together so last minute, we wouldn't ask unless necessary." Sergeant talks with Fowler sat on the side lines this time, heart in his throat wondering what is happening to Hallie. Sergeant has a photo or Hallie on the screen as well as Sebastian Chandler's drawing next to hers.

"Detective Hallie Jones has been taken by the same person who has been committing these killings." From this the room begins to stir, shock on their faces and notepads now out. Focus comes back to Sergeant quickly as soon as he talks again.

"Our top priority is to find Detective Jones alive and well as soon as possible. Time frame she was taken was approximately between 3-4am last night. Hallie was hit so she is wounded to what extend we do not know. She was carried into the suspects' car and driven to the abandoned Butterfly manor which is a 15-minute drive from where she was taken. We believe the suspect changed cars and has her in another location. We want everyone on board and working hard, need cameras checking, license plates checked, get this man's name and face out. We are unsure whether he still looks like this as this is a drawing from one of the victims who he be-friended. I have put a brief pack together for everyone, details of the suspect and Detective Jones for those who don't know her. Any information you get or have please come straight to either your superior who will contact me, straight to me or straight to Detective Fowler." Fowler's head looked up in shock when he heard his name, he has been zoned out for most of this meeting. "I won't keep you, this is now top priority, whatever you have been working on before this is now ahead, and you are to put full focus on. We have asked for you here today as the people in this room are some of the best of the best. We will find her, but communication is key. Thank you, you are all dismissed."

Chairs grinding across the floor everyone begins to leave, Sergeant is speaking with some of the higher-ranking officers and Fowler begins to head back to his office when he is stopped by Gibb.

"Hey mate, how you holding up?"

"Shit really, I'll find her."

"I know you will, we got this. I got us both a coffee maybe you could use a fresh set of eyes to look through some of the bits you already got?"

"Yeah, okay can't hurt." Fowler wanted to be alone, he didn't want to entertain anyone but at least Gibb is a smart man who won't talk shit and go on when you don't want to talk. He got the message Fowler was hurt, he wanted to help as he was also close with Hallie.

"I can't imagine what your mind is thinking right now." Gibb hesitantly says whilst going through Hallie's laptop to see if there is anything he can find that can give a clue.

"It is going a hundred miles an hour and then freezes then goes again. He took her, right under my fucking nose. I can't get over how he got in."

"She was with you?" Gibb looks up, that wasn't in the brief that they were together. No wonder he was cut up about it.

"Yes, she must have got up in the night and that is when he took her. I was asleep but if I woke up any earlier, I could've stopped it."

"You can keep going with the what if's and how's now Adam. You can't change what has happened. It is what is it is now and now our mission is to find her. If he wanted her no matter where she was, he would've taken her. You can't blame yourself." Gibb was young but he had a wise head which has somewhat helped Fowler.

"I promised her, I fucking promised her that she was safe, and no one would touch her, now look." Fowler stood up, his anger beginning to rise again.

"And now you will be the one to save her and catch this dick head who thought he has a chance. Then she will be safe. We need to focus Fowler is there anything Hallie was working on which took interest in this case?" Gibb was trying to keep Fowler's mind at ease and distracted, he knew everything about this case and what was going on. Now he needed to sit down and focus.

"Yes, the paperwork she found in Parker's top draw; it was locked. It was like a diary entry no idea who's. Here." Fowler handed it to Gibb, and they began to read through it all.

30

11am

Hallie knew as soon as she broke his camera, she would be in for it. She heard the footsteps almost instantly after she broke it. Attempting to slip from the handcuff before he got to her room, she nearly broke her hand. She couldn't quite get it off and was too late as the key was already in the lock. Hallie accepted this defeat and quickly sat on the floor and waited for whatever she was about to endure.

Sebastian walked in closed and locked the door behind him. He looked over at the broken camera, grabbed the metal chair again and sat down opposite Hallie. "Thought you would not like the camera. Least gives me more of a reason to come check on you now." His voice still calm, wondering what Hallie would have to do to make him snap like he used to.

"Well, aren't I lucky." Snorting at the idea he was watching her.

"What do you want to know Butterfly?" It was like Seb had read Hallie's mind. He knew she had questions but refused to ask them to stay strong and un-bothered on the situation.

"Why, are you different, before any opportunity you had you beat me, hurt me. Now you, I mean you still hurt me and kidnapped me but before was it so you could act all strong in front of your terrorist friends? And why did you kill them, did you kill the people 5 years ago or just these three?" Hallie had loads of questions but stopped at these ones, for now.

"I was hurting before, and when I knew you was on that mission, I had to make myself clear to your little team, that I could get what I wanted no matter how much they try and hide you."

"Hide me?" confusion spread across Hallie's face. She worked for special forces in the army, she was briefed on all meetings before a mission. Was he lying?

"Yes, they had been after me for about six years, your little team. I went under the radar after a mission I had done. Anyways, your team the year before you joined it killed my only family I had. Guess who pulled that trigger with no remorse?" Seb wanted Hallie to answer but she remained silent.

"It was your little sleeping buddy. Adam Fowler. Anyways, when I found out you had joined the team and was out on mission had to do a bit of investigating myself on you. You had no one, no family, no friends just the army to call home. Like me. I had no one. But I knew how Adam felt against you, the way he looked at you on missions and going undercover on one mission the way he spoke about you, well some wasn't very nice. At first, he thought you wouldn't be strong enough on the team and he tried to ruin your chances to stay, I think it was because he had a little crush on you, I mean who wouldn't." He paused to look Hallie up and down, realising she was still silent and undecided if she was to believe him. "Anyway, when Fladhir and his team took you, I went in to make sure you were strong enough. I will be honest, back then my head was full of revenge and wanted Adam's head on a stick. But you were the way I could get that. I used all the anger I had against Adam on you, because you still spoke highly of him, even though he held you back. He was the reason you didn't get on the team straight away; he made a bet that he would be the one to get with you and be your 'first bang'. He was horrible and I felt sorry for you Butterfly."

Hallie was silent, she couldn't believe that Fowler would do this, she wondered why she was held back so long before getting on the team. Maybe that was the reason, but then a sudden thought came across her mind, how could she trust the person who just kidnapped her and knocked her out.

Hesitantly, she responds. "So why me, why take me when you are so sure he didn't like me? Why did you choose to torture me and kill Ashira?"

"I killed Ashira because she worked with Fladhir, she was a insider and gave him all the information he needed on you. You trusted the wrong person there. When they said she was taken to be interrogated and beaten, she wasn't. In the end, I didn't want to hurt you, that is when I killed Ashira and left the building when your little rescue team came. I could've taken you; we could be working together now! But instead, I played the long game and made sure I would get you back, Butterfly."

Every time he said Butterfly, Hallie's stomach sunk, she was uneased by it. But was hooked on his story. Now she wanted to keep him talking, the more she got, the more he would think he trusted her, he might let her go, she could kill him and escape. All in good time.

"So why kill Katie, Alex and Parker. All part of the plan?"

"Now this is where it gets interesting, I read up on the case you had all those years ago, Nightstalker it was called. Anyways you did convict the right person, he killed the people all those years ago, but I did my research to make you both second guess yourselves, that you got the wrong person. I enjoy playing games, and watching you work was nice to see. I done my history on the building and found your mother there. Well, she's dead now, don't think you knew that. But she was like my mum, used me and hurt me until I got away. We are more similar than you think. Back to the story, when I went snooping around the hospital, met Katie and Parker, sweet girl but she was spoilt so didn't like that. She was planning on taking all her parent's money and running away with Alex. That was the real reason him and Parker fell out, Parker became a Dr because Katie's parents helped him get there. He felt like he owed them. They were all pretty fucked up, Parker used to drug his patients to make them sleep all day on his shifts, so it was easier, Katie was a spoilt brat who was planning on stealing everything her parents had, she was the reason they gave up there son. She lied as a child saying James hurt her when he didn't. James died in the hospital from Parker's mistake of giving him a drug to make him sleep but gave too much and killed him. He had done this a lot with a few patients. You see Butterfly, I don't kill people for fun, I kill them if they have done bad things and are better off dead." Seb still sat upright on his chair, no movements from him or Hallie. She still didn't trust him, but maybe he is telling the truth.

"So, why have you taken me. Must have a reason, if you kill people because they have done bad things, why take me?" Hallie knew she would get an answer from him, and this would be an answer if she was going to live or be killed.

Seb stood up and walked over to Hallie and crouched next to her. Hallie shuffled back but her back was now against the wall, she was unable to escape. "Because Butterfly, you are mine. Not his. He took what was mine, and your little lover has plenty of secrets. But he used you, I wouldn't. At first, it was for revenge. Now you will learn more about me, learn to like me, but now I can see it will take time. I went the wrong approach but learn I am doing this one, because I want you and two, to see Adam Fowler dead."

31

3pm

It has now been 12 hours since Hallie has been taken. Fowler has been working nonstop through the evidence they have and now has the photos and print outs of what the killer had sent through emails laid out in time order. Sergeant also joined them in the office to go through any evidence when Gibb finds something. "Fowler, did Hallie mention why random words have been circled?"

"She didn't know, was trying to figure out why, if the person that wrote it done it or someone else. Why?"

"Well, the torn off bit at the bottom, did you ever find it?"

"No, we didn't"

"Only suggest as this is the same writing as this person." There was a file on Hallie's birth mother and had her name written on the bottom signing her name as her discharge. It is her writing.

"The person who wrote this, it's Hallie's mother. Are you sure?" Fowler left his desk and went to join Gibb to double check.

"Positive, I put some words into this generator on my laptop, also remember seeing her name thought the writing looked similar and it's matched. So, why was this in Parker's draw?"

"I have no idea, do you think Parker remembers Hallie's mum and found the diary, to hide it when we had a warrant?" Fowler began to question all the why's for this. But why the random circled words? This was until he received a email.

"How did this fucker find out I was using this laptop?" Sergeant and Gibb both looked confused as they walked over and looked over Fowler's shoulder to see what he was talking about when they read the email.

> 'Did you really think I wouldn't be able to find you if you used a different user. You really aren't as smart as people make you out to be. I will give you the chance to find your partner but by my rules. I have given so many clues so far and you still not figured any out. Let me help you, K. A. P. All the first letters of the victims. The lives that have been taken. However, they are also the initials of locations linked with your partner Detective Jones. Let's see if you really know her like you say you do.

"I'm running track on it now see if can get any insight where it has been sent. Fowler, think. What is linked with Hallie to them letters?"

"It could be anything, fuck. Okay K. Location beginning with K?" Fowler was pacing trying to think.

"Fowler, he's sent you something else." Sergeant opened the email and read it aloud, no time to waste.

> 'If you figure this out, you will get the next clue. I will give you three clues in an attempt to find her. I want you to suffer like you made me suffer. We will meet, eventually Detective."

"Made him suffer, Fowler, do you know this man?" Sergeant had a stern tone, this made him question has Fowler got something to hide.

"No, I don't. I didn't see him on the mission in Afgan when he took Hallie, I didn't recognize him at all when you first handed us the drawing. I have no idea what the connection would be? Is it because I rescued Hallie from him on the mission?" Fowler was trying to figure out the connection between them and he couldn't.

"Well, let's come back to that. What is this location beginning with these letters that link with Hallie?" Gibb trying to get the focus back. He was already tapping away at all locations beginning with these letters in the perimeter.

"Could it be something will all the letters in or all separate locations?"

Gibb was already looking up on his system everything that had these three letters as the title. Until on match seemed more likely.

"Kurt and Peter's?" Fowler stood up and looked at Gibb who had just loaded the same answer.

"What is that?"

"It's a shooting range, Hallie goes there to let off steam, the owners are very friendly with her they have been since Hallie came back from the army. We need to go there." Fowler already grabbing his jacket and heading to the car with Sergeant. Gibb stayed behind to try de code the email and see if any other evidence they had could help figure out where Hallie is.

32

5pm

Hallie still had no idea how long she had been here, no sense of time or date as she doesn't know how long she was on conscious for. All she knows is that it feels like forever since she has been here. Seb comes back in with a takeaway and sits on the floor with her, slides her some food and a drink. Hallie hesitates at first but then takes it, but before she does, Seb released her from her handcuff.

"Hope I can trust you not to do anything you will regret Butterfly."

"Hope you can stop calling me butterfly and let me eat!" Hallie began with a drink from her mouth being so dry and then bit into her burger.

"Even eating you are beautiful" Seb couldn't take his eyes off her.

"You are a first-class creep, aren't you?" Hallie met his eye line but carried on eating. For the first time she didn't feel afraid.

"One of a kind." Seb joked.

"So, you this nice to everyone you kidnap?"

"Only the ones I want to keep."

"Let me get one thing straight for you, I am not property, you do not get to keep me, I don't even know you. Plus, you are a killer, a murderer, I have no idea how many people you would've killed?" Hallie began to tuck into her chicken nuggets, Seb had gotten a big selection of food.

"Do you?"

"Do I what?" Hallie looked up in confusion and Seb placed his burger back in the wrapper, lent forward and asked Hallie again.

"Do you know how many people you have killed? I know it is a big number having done what you have done as a job."

"That is different, you are a murderer now."

"You could say that, or you could say I am doing good in the world, getting rid of all the bad nuts."

Hallie looks back up at Seb, thinking is he serious, does he really condone killing people as a good thing. Hallie did notice that he hasn't locked the door behind him this time, she could make a be-line for the door.

"Stop that!" Seb snaps at her and her gaze meets his again.

"Stop what?"

"Planning how to get out, you can leave this room when you finally trust me."

"I won't ever trust you, everything you have done to me, and even now. All for what?"

"Time will tell. I am very persuasive. Anyways, how's the food?"

Hallie wanted to say it was vile, horrid, that she would spit it all over him, but it would be a lie. She knew it was good food as she hasn't stopped eating. Not wanting to give him the satisfaction she shoots him up a fuck you look.

"I'll take that look as it is good. Don't get me wrong Butterfly- "

"Stop calling me that!"

"What do you want me to call you? I like your name, but I prefer a nickname if I'm honest."

"Why, just use my name."

"Because, when I use your name is when you are in trouble. But nicknames, seem, happy." Seb began to clear up the empty food boxes and put back in the bag just leaving the large drinks.

"Well, you're still prick in my eyes." Hallie looked up and gave a sarcastic smile.

"Then you can be my thorn." Seb looked up and had a grin spread across his face. He had a perfectly symmetrical face and Hallie wonders how someone that good looking ended up this fucked up.

"Thorn, really?"

"Yes, every time a thorn pricks you, you remember it, the pain. That is how you make me feel now."

"You are fucked up."

"Maybe so, but aren't we all?"

Seb stood up and took the remains of the food with him. He was so tall and well built, no wonder why Hallie couldn't escape his grip, he is a tank. Hallie had to focus, she was now unchained and needed to get out of here. But the same thought kept going through her mind, why did Fowler do all that stuff.

Hallie was still in his t-shirt which she brought up to her nose to smell, she still could smell him on her. Shame the dark grey t-shirt was now stained with her blood. She could really do with a shower, bed. Maybe this is another nightmare. Wish it was.

Just three rooms down from where Hallie was, there was a large office. Seb went back onto his laptop and hacked into the security footage of the KAP shooting range to see if they took the bait, he does plan to give them a chance, but not until Hallie knows every bit of information on her partner she insists on trusting loving and fucking. Seb's blood begins to boil, knowing they had slept together made his skin crawl. Seb was possessive and he truly believes Hallie was his and she would fall in love with him. It takes time. And the person she loves is a liar and Seb couldn't wait to tell her everything he has done. Maybe when they come to rescue her, she will say no and stay with Seb. This is what he hoped. He went into another large room next door and double checked the windows, checked the strength of the doors, nothing could be used a weapon. We will give it few more hours, then see if she still behaving and offer her a bed to sleep in.

Hallie still going crazy in the other room. Beginning to pace and wonder if she will ever be found. Was this just Seb trying to get into her head, was it true, was Adam lying to her. She has always struggled to trust anyone, but she trusted Adam, was that a mistake. Hallie was beginning to lose hope in Adam but needed to remember, this sick fucker played mind games for a living, he is a trained killer. If he wanted her dead, she'd be dead.

Hallie looks down and sees her scars on her legs from years ago. She sees her scars as failures, a constant reminder and this person that has her all to himself, he was the one who put these scars on her body.

Who is to say he won't do it again. Fuck, concussion, mind games Hallie just began to curl up into a ball and began to cry herself to sleep.

Seb went back into the room a few hours later once he had taken care of a few things to see Hallie curled up in a ball asleep, he had an argument in his mind with himself, one side saying pick her up and put her in a bed, the other leave here she is bait. He let one side win, curled Hallie into his arms and carried her to a room which he had checked over few hours earlier. Hallie was sound asleep and didn't even stir when being moved. Seb kicked himself for being too kind-hearted, but maybe this is the I'm sorry Hallie could understand from his point of view. He tortured and abused the wrong person all those years ago. He wanted Adam, he took Hallie thinking of Adam and now look, he is growing feelings for Hallie. Carefully placing Hallie on the double bed and pulled the duvet over her body to stop her from being cold, inhaling her sent which was intoxicating. Resisting any urge he has for her he moves some hair that has fallen over Hallie's face and tucks it behind her ear and leaves the room locking the door behind him.

Seb gets into another car that he has stored in the garage below and speeds out the driveway. Heading back into the heart of the town knowing he is unlikely to be spotted as the photo the police have of him looks nothing like him. Yes, he still looked good but so much has changed and he is grateful for this. Seb planned on keeping Hallie but giving her the chance to find out the truth of her past and to want to stay with him. Knowing it would take a lot for Hallie to trust him given their past he was a patient man that knew what he wanted.

Arriving back at the house his shopping already been delivered, Seb packed all the contents away, went into his office to check the security footage before heading to Hallie's room. Opening the door to still see she hasn't moved a muscle and still is fast asleep. Resisting the urge to go closer to her, Seb closes the door slowly and heads down to the basement of his manor. Much to his surprise, his victim is somehow still alive, for now.

33

The shooting range was empty, past closing time but Fowler had a direct number for the owners. The owners live about five minutes away from the range which was helpful as they came straight away to unlock and allow Fowler and Sergeant to roam around.

"Why don't you ask me a question Fowler, anything. Try ease your mind and distract it a bit?" Sergeant looked over noticing Fowler still hasn't spoken much since Hallie's disappearance.

"Huh? Sorry, what's up?" Fowler's tone stern but disheartened.

"What do you want to know about me Fowler, distract your mind from thinking it is all your fault when you and I both know it is not."

"Yeah, uh okay. Why do we call you Sergeant? I mean it isn't it meant to be chief or something like that?" Fowler still not making eye contact and looking around for any clues that may have been left.

"It is because I didn't want to be Chief, I recommended to keep my title from the army and when I joined the force most people new me as Sergeant, just a name that has stuck. My real name is Albert, but Sergeant for you." Sergeant looks over and smirks at Fowler who returns the smirk. "Okay my turn, Fowler, I know you have had feelings for Hallie for a long time, when was you going to tell me about the two of you?"

"After the case, we didn't want it to affect the case or allow people to think or question us that we are still able to work together."

"I'm not mad at you both, I'm happy been routing for you both, she's a strong woman and if I care for her a lot. We will find her Fowler, the best teams out looking and all internal departments, we got this."

"That is the issue sir." Fowler finally met Sergeant's eye line, which caused them both to stop looking around for clues.

"What's the issue?"

"She is strong, too strong sometimes, it has taken her all these years to admit what he did to her, she keeps things to herself and bottles it all up thinking she can handle it, but she sometimes just breaks. Only recently she has been able to have full night sleeps without a nightmare from him or something of her past. She has been to hell and back sir, but I promised her that I would keep her safe and no one would ever hurt her and now look." Fowler soon after began to look around for clues again, he didn't expect a response but was something that needed to be said.

The range was dark and cold this time of night, walking around the corridors, each room had a different use. Fowler ignored the idea to check every room and headed straight to Room 7b. This room was a line target room, use of any firearm and was the only room Hallie and Fowler would use to train and let off some steam. Gladly, there was something in this room. As expected, as soon as the lights flickered on one of the paper boards that was hanging in the distant, however even from here you could see it had been shot. Sergeant presses the button which alerts the chain on the ceiling to pull the target closer to the shooter to check their hits. However, this one was hit exactly at the heart multiple times, then looking around the room shots are beginning to be fired. Both Fowler and Sergeant duck behind the unit, the shooter is stood where the target was before being brought in.

"Sarg, you, okay?" Shouting over the shots to check and attempt to reach for his weapon without being seen.

"Hold your fire, that isn't a gun shot?" Sergeant began to stand and noticed a banger at the back of the room with the fire door slightly open, whoever set this off didn't close the door behind them. The banger was meant for outdoor uses so this being inside was causing so much noise that it was almost deafening. Trying to avoid the sparks flying off the banger, Sergeant and Fowler headed for the back fire door and called for backup. Fowler ran ahead of Sergeant and headed for the back woods. He could hear Sergeant in the distance calling for him to hold up, but he saw red, Fowler's army training kicked into his head, he needed to run and run fast to catch up with whoever it was that had it out for him. Then he heard a scream, instantly thinking it was Hallie he ran faster towards the noise. Shouting for Hallie it wasn't until he realised, this could be a trap, and it was. There was a cabin and Fowler was alone, he had two options, wait for backup to arrive to check the building out, option two, to check the building alone. Of course, he knew he was going to go in alone, he has faced some shit situations, but this was beyond unexpected. He walked into the cabin's door and a TV was on with footage being played. The footage was of Hallie, asleep on the concrete floor, she wasn't moving a muscle to then be carried out by Seb. This video was played on a loop, which Fowler couldn't keep his eyes off, Sergeant soon arrived shortly after and watched the video along with Fowler. "Right, search this cabin, find the feed for this, and get the surrounding areas checked. He couldn't have gone far." Sergeant ordering his team whilst Fowler was fixated on the video still, he couldn't help but think the worse. Where he could be taking her, if she is hurt, what has he done to her. Now after seeing this video, his mind has shifted, he was ready to kill whoever this person was.

"Fowler, come take a look at this." Sergeant was at the back door of the cabin looking over the fields to which Fowler stood and joined him. "One of the team found another message for you in the forest." Handing over a piece of paper which had been crumpled up and a single hole through the top which must have been where it was nailed to the tree.

'Well done, you must know her somewhat. Too bad I know her better. As you can see, she is alive, but it does feel good seeing you suffer Detective. This cabin had some meaning behind it, but of course wouldn't make it that easy for you.'

"Is that it? Nothing else?" Fowler began to head back into the cabin to re watch the video see if he recognised the location or if Hallie gave any hints if she knew she was being recorded.

"We have taken the drive which has this video on loop, will give it to Gibb see if he can get anything from it. Looks brand new so maybe bought recently and can track him that way. He can cover most of his tracks, but not them all one will appear out the blue. Come on, let's head back." Sergeant tapped Fowler on the shoulder, it was late, he needed to sleep but he knew that sleep wouldn't happen anytime soon. Hallie was his priority, and he didn't want to rest until she was safe.

34

"Please, I beg you, please what do you want from me. Ok-Okay, I have money, whatever you want you can have it. Please just let me go!"

"Now, now. If I wanted your money, I would've had it all by now. You are what I want and if I am being honest, I am very surprised that you are even awake. True fighter." Seb begins to walk over to the man who was hanging from the ceiling by chains. His face bloody, broken nose, fractured eye socket, shirt and trousers ripped and could begin to see the bruises forming around his stomach. He had been tortured a few hours prior and is still able to talk which impressed Seb. "Now, seeing as you are chattier than what you were earlier, I will ask my questions again."

"Who even are you? You are a dead man walking if you don't let me go." The man tried to speak with force, but his voice cracked from the amount of pain he was in.

"Oh, you don't need to know who I am, I need to know who else you have working for you in your little establishment?" Seb dragged a chair to sit in front of the victim and looked him in the eye. He noticed he must've done some damage to the man's right eye as was bloodshot and puffy from all the swelling. Seb didn't quiver, making sure he remained eye contact he was determined to get information.

"I have no idea what you are talking about?"

Seb then began to press into his rib cage which was clearly broken, and the man screamed from the pain, tears forming in his bloody eyes attempting to breathe through it but that just caused him to be in more pain. "I won't ask again." Demanding this time to make sure some sort of answer is given.

"I don't know, honestly, I was in the wrong place at the wrong time. I was invited by Charlie Henderson who told me it was a formal gathering, I didn't know what it was, I really didn't." The man whimpered as he spoke from true fear of what Seb might do with him next.

"Now, was that so difficult. You can go now." Seb pressed a large button on the side of the wall and began to walk to the door.

"Just like that? Yo-You don't want anything?"

"Just one thing Thomas, you still helped to kill my brother. My only family I had so" and just like that Seb had shot the man directly at the centre of his head. Blood began to pool out as he led there, Seb thought about torturing him more, but he had had a busy day so easier just to get it over with. Leaving the room, he will deal with the body tomorrow for now to check on his little guest.

Heading up the stairs he realised he needed a shower, reminisce of the forest, gun powder from the banger and now the remains of young Thomas on his body he thought best to shower before checking on Hallie. Didn't want the stench to wake her, also to get more questions from her as to what he had done. Seb was sure he would win Hallie over, and to this was by far the best way to torture the man he hated, steal the love of his life, tell her all the truths he hasn't told and allow her to fall in love with him. Long winded plan, but Seb was obsessed with Hallie, somewhat more than killing Fowler which has been top of the list for years.

Seb unlocked Hallie's bedroom door and slowly opened it seeing the duvet all crumpled up. Stepping in to notice Hallie wasn't in bed but by the side of the door and beginning to swing for Seb. She took two attempts which was both missed by Seb's quick movements he managed to grab both of her arms and span her around, so she was in a lock, unable to move from the restraint and force Seb had given her. "See someone has had a good cat nap?"

"Why am I in this room?" Hallie still attempting to struggle from Seb's bear hug.

"Thought you would prefer a bed rather than a concrete floor, can move you back if you prefer but you looked better in the bed." Seb lifted Hallie into his right arm still in restraint to lock the bedroom door, he knows her abilities and she was quick so could get out quick.

"The bed is, nice but still confused why I am in a bed well a normal room if you have taken me and won't let me out?" Hallie realised she wouldn't be able to get out of this restraint so needed to stop struggling and accept this defeat, beside her headache was slowly coming back.

"Because, eventually you won't think of it as me that has taken you and accept it here." Seb still holding her tightly unsure of the response she might give.

"You, you think you're going to keep me. Like a fucking pet, absolutely not, would rather slit my neck."

"You'll learn to trust me, it will take time, but you will."

"Bullshit!"

"You calm enough yet that I can let you go, I mean would happily hold you all day, but I know you like your space."

Hallie sighed, how he knew that was unsettling like he had been watching her for a long time. Nodding in agreement to be let down.

"I didn't hear any words my little thorn?"

"You really sticking with that name?"

"Well, butterfly was the one for me but has some bad past so a new one is helpful."

"Just put me down."

"Could at least ask nicely then might consider it?" Seb knew teasing her was a bad idea but couldn't help himself, he loved seeing her no matter how she was.

"Oh, please kind stalker, please let me down so you can carry on staring at me, and I will still be trapped here."

Even in that tone was a slight turn on for Seb, "well, seeing as you asked so nicely there you go." Releasing his grip Hallie fell and walked back over to the bed, she knew she wasn't getting out yet, but her head was pounding so needed to sit down.

"What do you want with me?"

"You, I just want you, before was about revenge but like I said before, you deserve so much better Hallie. He will still suffer knowing he let you slip from right under his nose, but I want you to learn the truth about him." Seb moved forward and lent against the bed frame post. He towers over Hallie and looks even taller whilst she is sat down on the bed, I mean for what stalkers and kidnappers do look like least hers wasn't a sight for sore eyes. She observed him, all his little attributes like the slightly damp hair which looked towel dried and spiked up slightly but looked soft as a feather, then his t-shit which was slightly see through you could see the outline of his toned body with a dark line going down from his shoulder down his chest which Hallie has determined must be a scar.

"What truth?"

"All in good time, you need some rest then when you wake up can have some food and pain meds." Seb began to walk back to the door and hooked out the keys from his trouser pocket when a comment Hallie makes stops him.

"Are you jealous or something?"

"Of what?" still staring at the door.

"Of Adam, that he has me, that he is successful, that we both are." Seb turns around and Hallie is stood up off the bed and she is edging closer to him but stops about four steps in. "That he has had his hands over me in a way you never will. He cares for me and will find me. Are you jealous that he found me all those years ago and you still hold that grudge, are you jealous he has fucked me."

That was it, the keys back in Seb's pocket and he is storming over to Hallie, she stands her ground, but he is inches away from her face. Anger, rage, so many emotions that he is trying to control. "That's right, he has done all those things. But let me tell you one thing, he won't be laying a hand on you ever again okay. I don't even want his name rolling off your tongue."

"Or what, you'll kill me, torture me again?"

"No, you will learn your lesson even if have to teach it in other ways."

"You think I will ever think of you in that way you are wrong."

"Oh, you will darl, I know it, when you learn everything and you realise, I am here for you, I would do anything for you, but you are never to say anything about him again. Do you understand?" Seb still close to Hallie, he could smell her, he realised she was still in his shirt, that will change tomorrow she will have some of his clothes.

"I will always scream his name; I mean he fucks so- "

Seb grabbed Hallie by the throat not to tightly but enough to take her breath away slightly. "Don't think I won't teach you a lesson.

Thought you was in the army, good with commands. Maybe will have to jog that memory of yours."

"Fuck you" growling through but she could see that Seb was enjoying this.

"Do as your told darling." Slightly squeezing her neck tighter Hallie begins to have a rose blush flush across her cheeks. Eventually her stubborn ass gives in and says she will do as she told. It was a lie of course but anything to get him off her.

"See you tomorrow darl." Seb locked the door behind him and headed to his room, this had been a long eventful day. He popped his medications and laid on his bed thinking about Hallie and how long it would take to earn her trust, but he also couldn't help thinking how much fun that was, she is stubborn, and he will teach her a few lessons. This made Seb smile, knowing this is them bonding.

On the other side, Hallie laid in bed in tears, wondering why her and what the fuck is going on. The truth about Fowler, what truth, what lies has he told for someone to old that much of a grudge he has to take someone. To think, Hallie was finally getting comfortable with someone but that is just her luck. Her mind then went to Seb, she could see the hurt in his eyes when she spoke about Fowler, Hallie knew this would be the best way to torment him but to what extent will he go?

35

Waking up without Hallie by his side felt strange, like a part of Fowler was missing. But a new day, a fresh mindset from the hell he endured yesterday. Fowler managed to get a few hours of sleep however needed coffee to keep him on form for today. Sliding open his wardrobe he gets a fresh shirt and jeans on, going for a practical look as he has no idea what he would be enduring today. The news is on in the background and a witness appeal for Seb is now out in the open. Little does Fowler know Seb's appearance has changed so much that the photo they have shared is not like him at all. Grabbing a croissant from the breakfast bar and headed out the door. His house looked back to normal, no blood stains on the floor, no smashed photos lying around, but still had the feel that Hallie was hurt and taken from here. Fowler slammed the door closed and drove straight to the station, swiping his ID badge at the door he took the stairs to his office. Gibb had caught site of Fowler however he had his headphones in on loud, zoning everything out. Gibb caught up to Fowler and tapped him on the shoulder startling Fowler to spin around quickly, a fist clenched. "Woah- no need for that, just checking in with you." Gibb took a step back when he sees Fowler's reaction.

"Sorry, just made me jump that's all."

"Remind me never to surprise you again. Just coming up to your office, have some information on that drive you guys found with Hallie on."

"What information?" Fowler unlocking the office door about to enter however when the door opened it was not how he had left his office last night.

"What the- "

"I'll get Sarg, see if anyone had access to this office." Gibb pulled out his phone and called for Sergeant to get to Fowler's office asap. The office TV had a video of Hallie when she was tied up back in Afghanistan, about to be beaten.

Fowler steps into the office eyes gazed at the TV, there was photos of Butterflies around the room all a burnt orange colour, but that wasn't his concern, this video was. He was unaware on the extraction of Hallie that this was ever recorded. He had no idea there was cameras in the building.

The video shows Hallie being tied up by her hands which hung above her head, her head hung low until she looked up and was talking with Seb. She was beaten, she was strong, held it together but the video quality was clear, you could see the desperation in her eyes. Fowler couldn't not look away, even when Sergeant walked in his eyes didn't leave the screen, this is something he had never seen before only from what he had been told from Hallie.

"When was this, Fowler?" Sergeant was now stood next to him with Gibb to his left also watching.

"That was one of the rooms we found in the building for the extraction mission back when we both worked for special forces. Hallie told me what he did to her, but to see it is just- "

"He is playing us, isn't he?" Gibb was hesitant to talk, still shocked Hallie was still alive and talking after having her ribs crushed.

"Yes, he is. How the fuck did he get in here?" Sergeant pulled out his phone and called the security team who manage the ID entries and the cameras. "Yes, I need footage from last night, who was went in and out the building, the corridors and who has access to Detective Fowler and Detective Jones's office. Thanks" Ending the call Gibb took a step closer to the footage and was looking at the bottom corner of the screen.

"What is, that?" Grabbing his laptop and getting the video onto his screen to be able to zoom into the bottom corner and read what is there. "Here, look at this." He stops the video that has been on loop and switches it over to the white writing.

'I have everything, proof of it all. Well done for spotting this though, now

come find me, re-trace your steps. It is all there, if not you will have more than one death on your hands. Clocks ticking.'

Uncertainty filled the room; the silence was broken by Fowler's phone ringing. Unknown number which he answered.

"Detective Fowler speaking."

"Ahh nice to hear your voice. Now you get to hear mine. I know your phone is bugged so to everyone else listening hello to you also."

Fowler put his phone on speaker allowing Sergeant and Gibb to listen. He wasn't wrong, his phone was bugged for this very reason. "What do you want?" Fowler kept his answers short, but Sergeant looked over to encourage Fowler to keep him talking.

"Straight to the point, okay I will tell you. I want you to suffer, I want you to own up to everything you have done, I want you to know what it feels like to lose someone you love."

"Is she okay?"

"Can't even use her name can you. Yes, she is. But she is slowly learning the truth."

"What truth, you tortured her all those years ago and had it recorded. You killed innocent people for what, fun?" Fowler's temper was getting short, but Sergeant kept him calm, kept him from saying something he might regret. He needed to keep Seb in a good mood, or he could inflict pain onto Hallie.

"You're right and wrong in the same sentence. Yes, I did hurt her all those years ago, you know the lengths I will go. But you also need to realise you are the one I want to suffer."

"Then take me, let Hallie go and have me?"

"For you to play the big hero, absolutely not. You can prove you care for her by finding her. If I wanted you straight away, I would've taken you, wouldn't I. I can access anything and everything Detective and the sooner you realise that the better. Come find me, you prick." The line went dead. Fowler looked up from his phone straight to Gibb and Sergeant.

"What did you do to him to make him hate you this much?" Sergeant began to question a lot, this wasn't making sense, was it part of the sick game, if Fowler knew surely, he would've told them to help save Hallie.

"I have no idea, he knows me from the Army that much is all I know, maybe a mission but I don't recognize him nor remember his name. I have tried to remember, the part about owning up to the truths, what truths I don't know. Only lie I have told most of my adult life is my feelings for Hallie, look how that has ended up." Fowler went and sat on his desk and held his head in his hands. Gibb began to load up the information he found on the hard drive left in the cabin.

"Maybe this will help, I found this file on the drive also is a body cam footage video. Wanted to show you this before but, well anyways here."

"No, that was him, it can't be. No!" Fowler was in shock, he couldn't believe this, this had to be a trap or some CGI shit. That can't be real.

36

Waking up in a bed was nice, better than a cold concrete floor so Hallie wasn't complaining. Feeling like she must've been drugged last night as was a full night sleep which is rare for her, no nightmares, no random wake ups, no interruption. Nothing.

As she sat up to observe the room, it was a well decorated room, one that she would enjoy trashing out of spite for being taken. Head still slightly tender but loads better than yesterday. Noticing that some clean clothes lay folded on the bed she picked them up. As much as she wanted to keep Fowler's shirt on it would be nice to not be wearing a bloody shirt which would begin to smell if she kept it on any longer. Luckily this room had a bathroom, checking around she couldn't see any cameras, not that the sicko would make a hidden one somewhere. Realising she didn't care she headed to the bathroom, unaware of the day or what time it was, she noticed a fresh towel and a shower also in there. Taking full opportunity, she locked the bathroom door and turned the shower on. She knew she couldn't get her stitches wet so tried to avoid them but still trying to get the dry blood out of her hair. Hallie had beautiful long hair and she did not want it cut, the water was hot you could see the steam building in the bathroom. For the first time she felt somewhat normal, not like she was in some random building which was where she was kidnapped.

Wrapping her hair in the towel gently after drying her body she put on the clothes left for her. A pair of trackie bottoms which looked like they used to be bigger but had been shrunk down but still too big around Hallie's waist and a long t-shirt with Guns and Roses printed on.

As she went back into the bedroom, she found Seb just sat on the chair in the corner, hands held on each knee slightly crouched forward. This slightly startled Hallie, she attempted to just brush it off her shoulder, she had the towel in her hands rubbing her hair dry.

"Surprised didn't come perv on me in the shower, least that is a door I can lock."

"Thought you'd want your privacy."

"How very kind of you." Rolling her eyes still being sarcastic on the matter.

"I've come to check your stitches."

"Not got your little doctor here today then."

"Not today no, he was only here then because I knew you wouldn't trust me to do it."

"You got that fucking right."

Seb looked over to Hallie she sat on the edge of the bed, taking in the smell of shampoo and soap variety from her body. It was intoxicating seeing her with wet hair, he stayed sat down to try containing himself. "Can I check them then; I know you won't be able to."

"What makes you think I can't?"

"Because of the placement of the stitches, plus I would need to move your hair, and you have just washed your hair so make sure they haven't gotten too wet and need replacing. So, stop being stubborn and let me check them."

"Fine."

Seb stood up and Hallie followed him with her eyes, not moving a muscle noticing he is in the same comfy clothes as before she fell asleep. Seb on the other hands was enjoying Hallie in his clothes, slowly becoming his. Seb towers over Hallie when she is stood up so when she is sat down her head is right where his abdomen is, she can smell his aftershave on him but trying to focus on other things rather than his niceness.

He begins to gently move Hallie's hair out of the way to get a clean view of the stitches, he notices one is still slightly bleeding maybe she caught in the shower. He leaves her and heads into the bathroom to grab some cotton wool from under the bathroom sink, with some warm water to clean her wound. Hallie says nothing, just allows him to fix the problem he caused.

"Why are you doing this?" Hallie asks as he is dabbing her wound gently, she is trying to not make eye contact as it stings like a bitch. Thank God it is only water not alcohol or some sterile liquid.

"What do you mean?"

"Cleaning the stitches, letting me stay in a bed, have a shower, fresh clothes. Just confusing."

"I do care for you, sooner you realise that the better it'll be. I don't want to hurt you."

"So why take me in the first place?"

"Revenge at first but also to protect you. You would've found me from the killings I made before this, so I had to take you before you took me. He took you for granted and didn't care for you like you deserve."

"And you think you can?"

"Yes."

Still dabbing on the wound making sure all the stitches are okay and healing like they should. It has only been a day, but she looks like a fast healer at this rate. Any chance to touch her, Seb was going to take it.

"You said to me that Adam wasn't who I thought he was, what did you mean?"

"I will show you in good time, when you are ready to be shown. I have some things to take care of before then."

"So, what I just sit here like a lemon waiting until you decide when to actually tell me why I am here?" Hallie's voice was starting to raise.

"No, just, I want to keep you protected."

"You can't just wrap me in bubble wrap and call me yours, I am a big girl, have looked after myself all these years can keep doing it!"

"I know you can, but this is a lot to take in,"

"No shit"

"And I want to make sure you are ready, I'm sorry for what I put you through before, but I need you to realise I am doing this for you." Seb looked down and met Hallie's eye line, she broke contact first and began to look at her hands again.

"What day is it?"

"It is Thursday, when you were knocked out you was only out for a few hours, you have only been here for a day and a half I would say."

"How do I know you are telling the truth?"

"I wouldn't lie to you darl." Seb rolled up his sleeve and showed Hallie the date and time on his smart watch. Hallie looked and then looked back down at her hands.

"If I show you something, can I trust you to not do something stupid."

"I won't say yes or no, depends on what it is."

"Come with me." Seb heads over to the door and unlocks it. He allows Hallie to follow him, this could be her perfect opportunity to kick him in the nuts and run, but her mind was telling her to hold fire and find out what he knows. Outside her door was a long corridor, about five other doors on this corridor which made Hallie wonder if she was the only one here of if he had more victims hidden away. Hallie was a couple steps behind Seb carefully watching where he walked, to which the last door on the right was where they stopped.

"I hope this might ease your mind a bit." Seb opened the door and allowed Hallie to step into the room which was filled with monitors and screens. Somewhat like Gibb's office but seemed more extreme.

"What is this?" Hallie still shocked at the room, who would have this much technology.

"This is my office. The day I met you all those years ago I promised I wouldn't hurt you again and needed to change my mind set in the revenge I needed to take. Before I believed you was in on the mission which caused my hate to your partner. When I learned that you were not even on the team then made me regret ever laying a finger on you. I made sure I would get all information to show you. Here." Rolling out a office chair for Hallie to sit on she took the invitation as was intriguing to what he had to say.

Hallie began to watch the computer screen on the wall which Seb had images of Fowler on. "Your so-called partner was the one who delayed you going into special forces. He jeopardized any opportunity you had. You were the top of your regiment, but he didn't want you on the same team, working together."

"Why? And how do you even know this?"

"Because it is my job to learn anything about anyone I need to. It is what I am trained to do. I got as much information on the special force team that I needed to do and the lot of them were corrupted. They all done dodgy shit, makes me sick they was even able to be in the army.

Detective Fowler put in a negative form about you to ensure you didn't get on the team. It didn't work as your other little teammate Harris contradicted it and said how great you would be. He seemed like a real friend for you, but shame he died."

Hallie looked down at her lap, she still never mourned over Harris and always found it odd how he was shot in the room she was in when she was un- conscious.

"I didn't kill Harris; I killed the others but not Harris. My target was Fowler and the others."

"Can I ask something?" Hallie looked over to Seb who still stood at the back of the room.

"Sure"

"Why do you want him dead?"

"Because he killed my only family I ever had."

"When?"

"On a mission the year before you joined special forces, him and his team was on an extraction mission which went wrong. I was also on the same mission with who I am with now and my brother. We explained to special forces that we were after same person and same ending. Your buddy Harris was on board, the others were not. In the end me and my brother got the extraction, as we left someone had shot our back tyre which made us stop in transit. Was three of special forces and one was Fowler. Fowler instructed them to take the target as he shot me and my brother."

Hallie was in a state of shock, disbelief of what she was hearing. Why would he do this?

"But he knew you was all on the same side, right?"

"Yes, he took the glory with his team saying they done the extraction, and we were eliminated by the opposition. My shot was clean straight through, healed but he shot my brother in the chest causing him to bleed out on route. I swore I would kill him and make him suffer for a loss like I did." Seb was looking at the floor, that was the first time he had ever said that allowed since it had happened. Hallie could see his pain, she put herself in his shoes and sympathized with him.

"So that is why you took me, because he cares for me, and you know this would make him suffer."

"Yes. I didn't want to hurt you, but I did, I promised myself I wouldn't hurt you ever again, so I want to make sure you are comfortable and able to just be around me."

"It will take time to trust you, I still think you are a prick. But I do understand this. What I don't understand is why you still kill people?"

"Because, what I do I eliminate the bad because they get away with too much, the people I kill are all for a reason, the reason must be pretty big as to why they need to die. Most are some fucked up people that need to suffer before they die some just kill to get out the way."

Hallie was still so unsure on all of this; she has the military and the police force drilled into her head and this seemed so fucked up but somewhat logical, I guess.

"So, the reason for the three people you killed wasn't just for my attention?"

"Somewhat yes, but I knew you would solve it quick enough. They deserved to die they had done fucked up things that they kept doing after being warned." Seb finally looked up to Hallie who was so gazed by him. She saw him as this prick who kidnapped her, his reasons seemed somewhat valid.

"You could've done this in such a better way rather than just kidnap me."

"I could've, but no fun in that is there darl." A devious smirk spread over Seb's face which was one that still unsettled Hallie but hid her reaction.

"Will you ever let me go?"

"When you can trust me and I am done with what I need to do, yes but for now you are with me. Okay."

"Don't really have much of a choice, do I?"

"Not really, I want you to be happy. I want you to be loved by someone who doesn't lie to you and has your best interest at heart. Adam Fowler is not that man."

"And you believe you are?"

"Yes."

37

"You have to be taking the fucking piss Fowler?" Sergeant wasn't one to swear but this was something else. Even Gibb was still in shock, he had already seen the footage but he didn't intend on Sergeant seeing it but he would've found out anyways.

There is footage from Seb's hidden button camera of Fowler shooting him and his brother which the goes fuzzy soon after. The video itself describes everything that happened as to why Seb hates Fowler.

"I didn't know- I didn't see any cameras on him when we done checks. It was needed."

"Needed Fowler. Fucking needed. Well thanks to you being careless enough to shoot the man and whoever that is next to him you didn't shoot to kill him as he is now out to get you back. But well-done of getting Hallie dragged into your fucking mess." Sergeant was pissed, even Gibb flinched at when he spoke. Knowing Sergeant was being honest, this hit Fowler even harder. What more does he know. He was young back then; he is different now. He acts different now.

"That was years ago, that was the mission. I didn't trust them, and I was right as look what he is capable of now." Fowler was still watching the video of him shooting Seb thinking what he would be doing to Hallie to make her pay for his mistakes.

"You shot him. Like he wasn't armed, and you shot him Adam." That was the first time Sergeant had ever called him his first name. Hallie was the only one to use his name.

"Because he had the target, that was our extraction."

"Don't give a shit, if that was the case, should have made sure he was dead. Because he now has one of my team hostages and it is on you now. Go back, follow what he suggested, re-trace your steps hopefully he will do as he says and let us have Hallie unharmed and alive. This is a big fuck up Fowler, I got to go make a few calls." Leaving the room allowing the door to slam behind him both Fowler and Gibb knew that he was not happy with this. If this ever got leaked out Fowler could lose his job, could lose everything.

Gibb was speechless, he removed the drive from his laptop and began to load up what he had been working on yesterday to try distracting them from what has just happened. "Urm, so I got some more information on that hospital and the victim that was the doctor, he was already on his second disciplinary for neglect and administrating drugs unauthorized when he was a nurse. Looks like he cost the hospital a lot of money in lawsuits from parents and family members of the people who he did this too. Also, think you might want to know Hallie asked me to do some digging on the records of the hospital about her mum who was there."

Fowler finally took his eyes off the blank screen and directed himself to Gibb. "And what did you find out."

"Well, she overdosed around the same time Parker was going through his nursing degree with the hospital. He administered the drug however the record shows she had been clean for 3 years and on the mends, but because he administrated such a high dosage caused her heart to fail. The hospital had it covered up and was lucky too as she had no immediate family or anyone to fight her case. Sad really, she could've had a normal life after being clean all those years."

Fowler looked back over any notes Hallie left from the case, then looked back to Gibb. "Fancy a trip out."

"I mean, it's always nice to get out this place, where we going?" Whilst already grabbing his coat and heading out the door unknowing where they would end up.

"St Catherine's, you are going to hack their system and I need to check out something there. That room that was in the video keeps coming up in my head and wanna see if anything I missed."

"Sure, can we get coffee on the way though?"

"Feel like I need something stronger than coffee after all of that." After stopping off and getting coffee they headed straight to St

Catherine's to see it is now all boarded up. No residence, no staff, not a person in sight. Ideal for Fowler, less small talk for him as he was in no mood to talk uselessness to anyone. They went in through the door on the side which had not been boarded properly so easy access. Gibb went in with his bag around is shoulder carrying his laptop and hard drive. He began to look around the building questioning how this place ever looked nice.

"Looks bit different then from the photos?"

"It does, will have to take the stairs, the electrics have probably all been cut." Heading through the back lobby they headed for a stairwell, which as you look through the centre was a spiral of squares that never ended.

"Don't tell me the place we need to go to is the top floor?" walking up the stairs already breathless and hasn't even climbed three floors yet.

"Don't get out much then Gibb?"

"Nope, my only physical is when I have to run to your office and back to mine. Even that makes me tired."

"Well let's hope we don't have to run after anyone today then". Smiling to himself knowing that Gibb didn't think he would be in a chase or anything physical, just hacking. Soon after they arrived on the floor from the video, Fowler pulled out his phone to use the flash as a torch, the corridor was cold, and you could hear the wind whistling through the broken window. Rain battered against the walls of the building as the weather forecast a storm of high winds and rain. Opening the door to the old locker room, he knew instantly something was different as all locker doors were now closed. Maybe when the team came to do a sweep through, they closed it. Fowler began to open each one to check if anything was left in there to which he opened locker 7 to find a box.

"Nope, nope, na ah. I didn't sign up for creepiness Fowler, this is a trap, or something. I don't li- "

"Will you be quiet and take a breath. It is fine. We will photograph it, see the contents, and go from there." Fowler then lifted the lid of the box to find a pair of lungs with a note on the top.

"Nope, told you would be something fucked up, that stinks." Gibb had to take a step away as he didn't deal well with this at all.

"Good thing you are just the techy then. You get used to fucked up things the more you are surrounded by it."

"Nope think I'll pass on that; it is different than seeing it on a screen. Why they fuck is that in a box here?"

"They are one of the victims, all that was missing on the crime scene was his lungs. This was the one who worked here the Dr that was not a very nice person by the sound of it." Fowler picked up the box to remove it from the locker and get the note from it which was a postcard form. Had the same butterfly on the front, a but was more red then burnt orange this time.

'Finally following instructions, better late than never. Now it is time for you to work, your little Sergeant now knows what you done. Could let the whole world know, not yet.
00'76'82'18'93'5'

Gibb knew exactly what those numbers were, and he tried his best to ignore the smell and try not to throw up everywhere and focus. "These are co-ordinates, he is giving clues, least isn't a goose chase like the last one."

"Don't speak to soon, where does it lead."

"Back at the abandoned Butterfly Manor where he stored the original car Hallie was taken in."

"I'll call it in, come on."

"You're not bringing that in the car, are you?" Pointing at the box with the lungs in, Gibb began to jog slowly down the stairs behind Fowler.

"Yes, it is evidence, come on."

"I am going as fast as I can, I'm not as fit and healthy as you."

"Well, after this I am going to start to train you up."

"Yeah, solid pass on that, I will enjoy my skinny appearance and lack of sunlight if I can stay away from rotting corpse."

"We will see."

As they reached the bottom floor, they tried to open the door which took them to the lobby, it wouldn't budge. Fowler handed the box to Gibb who took it but soon put it back down and began to try and kick down the door.

"Fuck, what is blocking it?"

To which Fowler heard a ticking like in the shooting range, to turn around and find the same banger as before. "Run Gibb, up the stairs." Unsure he began to run, Fowler grabbed the box and followed him, for someone who didn't run or do any physical activities least he could run if his life depended on it. Fowler calls Sergeant to get someone to the building but has no signal.

"Shit, need try get some signal somewhere." To which Gibb pulled laptop and sent a location directly to Sergeant phone to signal to get someone to the hospital.

"See Gibb, you work well under pressure."

"Yeah, well I also work well from my chair too. If we get out of here, you're taking me to the other place, aren't you?" Gibb looked up over to Fowler who was gazing out the window and noticing a hooded figure stood on the front garden where the fountain used to be.

"Yes, I am." Responding to Gibb but not telling him what he has just seen as will only worry him more. This was a fight now, and Fowler was now determined to win it.

38

Seb gave Hallie roam of the halls on their way back to her room. Not only to check out her surroundings but to crush those thoughts going though Hallie's head like who else has he got hidden here. How could he possibly think that he would be a better match for Hallie, I mean they don't know each other, he kidnapped her, he had also beaten her. At least she had known Fowler since she was 16 and worked with him. That footage of him shooting Seb and his brother was a little bit too shocking for Hallie. It hasn't yet sunk in that part.

As she walked down the hallway, one door was locked that Hallie wanted to look in. As she turned to look at Seb, he was already looking down to her. Waiting patiently for him to pull out his keys and open the door she met his eye line. "Why is this one locked?" Hallie the proceeded to keep turning the doorknob knowing it wouldn't help unlock it.

"Because that leads to the basement, and I don't want you down there." Seb's voice was deep and husky, how he managed to make everything sound seductive was beyond Hallie, but she tried to force any of them kind of thoughts out of her head.

"Why? What do you hide down there?" Still turning at the doorknob

"I only use it for work related things. Very rare I am down there but right now I you're my concern."

"Do I know the person you have down there." Hallie wanted to rule out that he had Fowler tied up down there, or killing someone on the force to get information, too many things were going through Hallie's mind, so she needed to put that at ease.

"No, you don't know the person who is down there."

"Okay, they don't have a relation to me at all?"

"No."

"Then I will move on." Hallie released the doorknob and headed around the bend of the corridor to the kitchen, realising she hadn't eaten yet and somehow a kitchen made her stomach rumble.

"What do you fancy?"

"I can make something myself."

"If I was going to poison you darl, I would've done it by now." Seb headed over to the fridge and pulled out some ham, butter, and cheese. He made some toasties for them both, this was the most time she had spent with someone that wasn't Fowler and it didn't feel like it was her kidnapper more like a friend. Still aware of the circumstances and the situation she was in Hallie had to be mindful and not allow her mind to sway off track. She needed to get out of here, but she now wanted more information on Seb, and to why he has a obsession with her and still feels the need to kill Fowler.

"Here. I can make something else if you get hungry."

"Thanks." Hallie took a bite of her toastie, and her mouth filled with saliva. She didn't realise how hungry she was till now. Seb's kitchen was like a modern farmhouse, an island breakfast bar in the centre, a agar for an oven which was something Hallie was sat near as was like sitting next to a radiator, the cabinets were white wooden with silver handles and a set of hanging lights gracefully fell from the ceiling. He must have paid some money to have this done as it was something you would see in a magazine for some rich wife's house.

"Can I ask you some questions?" Hallie still mouthing down the last remains of her toastie, she didn't like to make eye contact too much with Seb, felt safer somehow that way.

"You can."

"Can you tell me about yourself, like personal. Seeing as you are not going to let me go any time soon may as well learn about who you are."

"So, you are slightly interested in me?" A snigger left Seb's mouth and he looked up at Hallie, swiping his hair out of his face and then getting up to make another toastie for them both, Hallie took her opportunity to get a good look at him in normal daylight.

"Don't get too full of yourself prick, only want to know about my stalker seeing as you already know about my whole fucking life."

"Feisty, okay what do you want to know?"

"Everything, childhood, teen years, how you became so fucked up. You know the general?" Hallie didn't want to insult him too much as she really did fancy another toastie.

"Childhood was shit, just me and my brother. Mum died when we were young, dad beat us, eventually got me and my brother out and dad got put in prison and died that same year. Teen years was okay, got in the forces, was little shit in school as was looking after my brother so missed a lot but was a smart kid, passed everything. Hacked the school system once got kicked out for that. Learnt about technology and also how to bulk up as was picked on as a kid for being too skinny. Went in the forces, improved my skills, brother soon joined, we worked together then went into our own company. Have people working for us on the side lines around the globe. That one mission cost so much to me and that was the mission my brother was killed." Seb didn't look at Hallie, he could sense she was staring at him, but he didn't want to look, he didn't show any signs of weakness in front of her.

"You already know my life don't you."

"I do. We have more in common than you think."

"Yeah, except I have never kidnapped someone or murdered anyone so think you win the fucked-up category on this one." Both Hallie and Seb laughed, this was the first time Hallie had seen a genuine smile leave his mouth. How could she be in such a fucked-up situation but feel somewhat okay with it.

"What was your brother's name?"

"Luke."

"Got a photo?"

Seb looked over shocked, why was she interested, why did she care. Was she finally warming up to him, did she comfortable enough around him, was she just digging for information as she is well known for her interrogation skills. He walked through the open arch beam and opened a cabinet draw and pulled out a small box. Placing it on the breakfast table he opened it and pulled out two photo frames. One of two young boys around 10- or 11-years old arm over each other and another looking like it is a reenactment of the childhood photo. This one she noticed more of Seb in, he was right he was a skinny child but in the older version photo he was bulked up as was his brother.

"I'm sorry you lost him. Can't imagine what that must've been like for you."

"Hard, but he will always be with me."

"I do understand your hatred, I mean if I had a sibling with a history like you both did, I would feel similar, but I still don't think murder is the right way to go."

Seb put the photos back but left the older version one out. He came back in and sat next to Hallie; she could smell his aftershave which was divine. He held the photo, "Bad people don't deserve second chances. He had too many and now is still doing bad things, he deserves to die. I know you care; you are human and have spent so much time with him over the years, but I will show you everything I have that proves he is not the person you think he is." Seb was now looking at Hallie, she noticed a scar across the top of his face but taking in the words that just left Seb's mouth finally hit her. What more things has Fowler done, and still.

"Then show me. I barely know you; how do you think I can trust you."

"Because you will learn to, you see the good in people and people take advantage of you darl. I want to make sure that never happens to you again."

"You cannot keep me. I am not your pet."

"When I show you everything, you will want to stay." Seb's hand moved towards Hallie's face and moved a piece if hair that draped across her face, gently tucking it behind her ear he cradled his hand behind her head. Too soon for him to make a move, he needed her to trust him not fear him. Hallie didn't shy away from this action, she let him do it. Soon after she went back to her room as a headache was forming, Seb suggested she go sleep it off. Agreeing, she went back to the room she was placed in and drifted off to sleep. This was beneficial for Seb as he had business to take care of and that business was rotting in his basement.

39

Knowing that both Fowler and Gibb were stuck in a stairwell wasn't the worse of the situation. Fowler began to think of an escape plan as smoke was beginning to come through from under the door. Encouraging them both to climb up to the next floor, then the next one, then the next, all to try and find a decent signal. Gibb had his laptop out and was regretting his decision to join Fowler on this little trip.

"Any luck?" attempting to grab anything to smash a window to allow air through the stair well, turns out it is harder to break through a glass window on a mental hospital.

"It has sent, I can't get a response, not to say they haven't responded. But no signal so can't view anything."

"Are you able to hack into any of the old data base here?"

"Nope, it is all coded, whoever has done this knows their shit. I mean, I would happily learn a thing or two from this person. Shame he is a psycho." Gibb realising what he had said looked up to Fowler to see him staring at him as though he was going to kill him. Gibb took this as a sign to stop talking and keep typing. Any way to hack a close mast tower which would hold a signal might help.

"How is this fucker still one step ahead all the time. Just doesn't make sense."

"Wait, your phone, it is still bugged right?" Gibb finally looking as though he knew something Fowler didn't.

"Yeah, I assume so."

"He has hacked our data base multiple times, who is to say he hasn't hacked your phone to be able to get a location of you, to get rid of all your security footage, to know when you would be home with Hallie to make the move. It all makes sense. Give me your phone!" Gibb took Fowler's phone off him and pulled out a cord which hooked the phone and laptop together. Typing away he soon stopped, his hands froze hovering over the keyboard like he wanted to do something but couldn't move. Fowler noticed this and stopped looking through boxes.

"What?"

"He is a very clever cookie."

"I'm sorry?" Fowler began to walk over away from the window and towards Gibb who still hadn't moved since.

'You really are the best in your division Gibb. Would have you working for me if I could. I will always know your next step, your next move, your next breath. You will never escape Adam. Enjoy'.

Gibb began typing again, loads of codes appearing on his screen to which he was adding to, removing numbers, letters he was typing so fast his fingers could fall off. Fowler walked back over to the window to see the familiar shadow standing there again. This time he waved then walked into the forest.

"Gibb, need you to use your words, words I'm going to understand as to what you are doing now?"

"He hacked the phone; he has done since it was bugged by us. He also hacked the nearest cell-tower to ensure we wouldn't have access to contact anyone. I have override this and in about 10 seconds we should have signal to call for back up."

"You Gibb, are a bloody genius you know that!"

"I know that. I also know that a little trip out with you is never a little trip out" Gibb looked over his glasses and smirked at Fowler still typing.

The ten seconds was up, both their phones began to alert through with messages. Fowler got straight back on the phone and got back up to their location asap.

Back at the station, Fowler began going back through all the evidence they had collected throughout this case. He knew something was missing. The next stop was the abandoned butterfly manor which didn't make much sense as was still cornered off.

"Fowler, my office now." Sergeant didn't even step foot in the office just headed straight back to his desk. Fowler stood up and looked over at Gibb who gave a reassuring look to him. He knew he was in the shit, and he put the one person he loved life at risk.

As Fowler entered the office he was greeted by his old Captain, Captain Brooks who did not look as happy as he did the last. Both Sergeant and Captain had the same facial expressions, and this was a make-or-break moment. They could remove Fowler from the case, could kick him off the force, anything but Fowler just stood with a straight face, trying not to show emotion and figure out what is going on.

"Detective, I have briefed Captain Brooks on these videos found from back when yourself and Detective Jones was in special forces. Needless to say, his response was similar to mine." Sergeant sat at his long desk with his arms folded and kept a firm eye contact with Fowler. All he could respond with at this time was yes sir.

"Why in god's name did you not tell me this. Any of this!"

"Sir, it was a last-minute decision myself and the team made to ensure the safety of the extraction."

"They both worked with your team Adam. But I guess you forgot that. Harris was not in this video, I am assuming you didn't tell him your little plan."

"No sir, Harris didn't know."

"That shows, you didn't tell your Commanding Officer that you were on a killing spree. Why? Why didn't you tell Harris?"

"Because he trusted them, the team and I had a bad feeling about them. Needless to say, gut instinct was right as look what he is capable of now." Fowler regretted saying this as soon as these words left his mouth. Captain Brooks stood up and he looked like he was about to pin Fowler up against the wall by his throat.

"Needless to say? Needless to say Adam hey. Because of you he tortured your teammate, because you and your lack of ability to shoot to kill, you killed someone he worked with and judging from the responses you have now that someone was very close with him. Because of you, he is taking out his revenge on Hallie because you showed you care enough for her, and he wanted to take something that you loved. If I am honest Adam, you don't deserve her. This this is unlike anything I have heard in the army, and I have been in it for some time. Understand this, this will now be added to your file."

"Ours too, you will still work the case as we need to get Hallie back alive and well but my god Adam you are treading on very thin ice. You put one step out of line I will make sure you regret it." Sergeant meant what he said. Fowler wanted to argue his case, thinking best to just stay quiet and agree was the right thing to do.

"I understand. I can only apologies, I did not expect it to turn out this way and I understand it is my fault. I take full responsibility."

"You are dismissed."

Leaving the office and heading to his own, Fowler slammed the door shut and through all the contents off the draws onto the floor. Pissed was an understatement to what he was feeling right now. Luckily, he was in the room alone and he was the type of man to not show emotion much but he broke. This was hard, he just wanted to know that she was safe. His career was on the line also but so was Hallie's life.

40

Hallie was back in her room, which wasn't her room, but felt more like her room than her actual room. Looking at the bed it had been freshly made whilst she has been out of the room, which means it isn't just her and Seb in the building. Hallie was still trying to take in all the information she had just been given and is so confused on who to trust and if any of this is true.

Meanwhile, Seb headed down the basement to which he was met by two men. The body that he had left there was gone, the room was clean, not a trace of blood in sight. Seb headed over to the back door and pulled it all the way shut. "Thank you, was getting round to that." Seb looked over to both the men and pulled himself a chair.

"Least we could do, wish we was here to watch it. What did he say then?" The man was shorter than Seb, around 5ft 7 but still well built. The other a similar height however looked in experienced in this department. He had a laptop resting on his lap as he began to type away.

"Do you have WIFI or something I can use; the signal is shit."

"I do, but don't let any random person use it. Hey Ward, who the fuck is this?" Seb was pointing at the man, he soon closed his laptop lid and realised he should have stayed quiet.

"Sorry man, he's new, breaking him in. This is Kayden, he has worked with me for about a year now. I trust him, so can you. He is, well he is getting there but needs to learn to keep his Fucking Mouth Shut." Ward shot a harsh look to Kayden which ensured he would shut up if he wanted to keep breathing. "Were we right?"

"Indeed, we need to move, and need to move fast. Got enough on my plate to be dealing with this going to shit as well."

"Ooo trouble in paradise."

"Could say that. Taking care of some personal business shall we say." Seb kept his emotions in check. He did not want to let on what he had going on especially with these two. Wade he knew well, served in the military with him, this Kayden though well he knew he would have a background check as soon as he is back upstairs.

"Well, here if need a hand with whatever that is? Anyways, happy to have him dead regardless so job well done I'd say. Kayden get in the car." Wade pointed to Kayden who nodded and walked straight out the door.

"Next time Wade. Don't bring random people here."

"I know, I messed up hence why thought I'd take this one. Here, thought you'd want to see this." Wade handed over a brown envelope which Seb opened whilst Wade was still there. Scanning over it he knew exactly what it was. It was one of the biggest targets they ever had, and one they had been waiting on the right time to take it.

"I'll call you; we need to think this one through. Charlie Henderson is one man who has a lot of enemies. Give Blake and Kat a call get them in on this. I don't want that kid on this though Wade, he can get trained on another mission, not this one. This one will, well we need to know he is ready and from what I can see he is not. Call me when they are briefed, we will arrange a meet to discuss steps. Understand."

"Yes sir, crystal clear. Will call tomorrow once all is arranged." Wade left the basement out the back door to meet Kayden in the car. Wade had worked with Seb for a long time, he had worked with Seb and his brother all those years ago. Wade was one of the only people Seb could say he trusted. But still was cautious on everything and anyone.

This news Wade had given Seb was big, but he had waited long enough to finish this business with Adam Fowler and needed a pick me up so headed straight to Hallie's room. He expects some sort of resentment, an argument at least, or even Hallie to be hid behind the door ready to pounce on him like a Panther. But to his surprise, Hallie was led on the bed, curled up into a ball with a single tear rolling down her face. Seb hated seeing her like this, he wanted to fix any problem, any issue she had to make her happy. He knew deep down that he could be the reason she is feeling this way. He went in anyways and sat on the edge of the bed, his eyes looked up to Hallie who was still looking at her knees. Finally realising she was not alone she looked up to Seb.

"He killed him, didn't he?" Another tear followed down Hallie's cheek but this time she looked Seb dead in the eyes. Seb maintained the eye contact with Hallie.

"Who do you mean."

"Harris." Hallie stuttered when she said his name. She never spoke about Harris not even to Adam because it was too hard. Their friendship was more like family, siblings as such. They got on so well and had each other backs. It was odd how he died but Hallie never asked to much about it as she wanted every memory of that time erased from her.

"Yes."

Three letters, one word that shattered Hallie. Whilst in the room alone her mind wonders and she realised how the story Adam had didn't add up.

"Why? If he wanted him dead, why did he help him out?" Hallie tried to keep her emotions in check, but this was getting too much for her to handle.

"So he could play hero in it all. I wanted to tell you at the start, but I didn't know how. I'm sorry darl." That was it, Hallie's tears were beyond her control now she cried into her knees to which she was pulled across into Seb. His arms wrapped around her whilst she cried, he understood her pain and just allowed her to let it all out. She never grieved Harris's death until now. Allowing herself to feel Seb's arms around her she slowly fell into his lap, never, she never allowed herself to trust anyone, and she slowly learned to fall in love with Fowler and for this.

Hallie now began to realise she was led in her kidnapper's lap, this was the person who hurt her so badly she had nightmares of him, yet right now she didn't want to be alone and wanted his company.

"Is there anything I can do darl?" Seb still holding onto her tightly wanting to take away any pain she has ever felt because of this man.

"Is this how it feels?"

"Yes, feels just like this. Not only betrayal but the truth. It fucking kills you inside, makes you feel so alone and so numb. It tortures you and makes you question everything. I was hesitant on telling you because I didn't want to hurt you anymore. I promised I wouldn't hurt you anymore." Seb now resting his head on the back headboard knowing he couldn't do anything to make this better. This took time, and time was something he had for Hallie.

"Well, you are still a prick for not telling me straight away. But thank you." A smile stretched across Seb's face, he wanted to stay in this moment forever. Hallie allowed herself to be vulnerable and show emotion in front of Seb.

"I'm sorry." Hallie sat up quickly and wiped the tears from across her face. Realising she was crying in the lap of her kidnapper was something she never expected.

"It's okay. I'm sorry I didn't get to you sooner."

"Instead, you insisted on playing a game" Hallie now was looking over to Seb and for the first time she saw a look in his eyes. A look only to describe as hurt, he was giving some emotion to Hallie as she did for him.

"I know you still don't trust me. But one day I hope you will. I do care for you."

"I understand" that was it. This was the first time Hallie didn't give a sarcastic comment or a fuck you. She was too drained for that, she wanted answers.

"You hungry, can order some food. Anything you fancy?" Seb still on the bed just in case Hallie needed him.

"I'm not that hungry really."

"Well, you need to eat. So, I will get us some food and go from there, you need something to line your stomach with for the pain meds. Okay."

"Okay."

Seb left the room but soon re-entered with a cup of tea and some more clothes for Hallie. Somehow, Hallie felt a warmth from him, still not sure whether to trust him completely but this was something else. Hallie took this opportunity to run herself a bath and just lay there. The hot water gave her security, being underwater, the silence that surrounded her was calming. Like she was in a world of her own, slowly opening her eyes underwater she enjoyed the peace, quiet until an image set in her mind of Adam shooting Harris which caused her to shoot up out of the bath, panting out of breath. Unsure how long she has been in the bath for she heard a voice from the bedroom.

"Hey, you alright?" It was Seb, he was back with food, which made Hallie realise she was hungry. Attempting to get out of the bath and get dried off so Seb didn't come in and see her scars. Her naked in front of him didn't really faze Hallie, it was the scars. She was embarrassed by them, not only the ones she got from Seb all those years ago but the ones she had from a child, from other people. Every scar in her eyes was a failure. So, the more covered she was the better she felt.

"Yeah, I'm fine, just slipped, I'll be out in a sec."

However, Hallie didn't realise the bathroom door was still slightly open so Seb could see parts of Hallie. Her body was incredible, well-toned, he watched as she dried herself all he could see was her back. Her little dimples at the base of her spine, and water droplets which glided down her soon disappeared when she placed a towel around her to dry herself. Seb tried to peel his eyes away and dish up the takeaway he had just ordered but he couldn't resist watching her. Watching his t-shirt fall down her body for it to hang just above her thighs and wearing his comfy trousers he knew they would smell like her from now on.

Finally, he snapped out of it and dished up their dinner, putting both plates on the desk he gave Hallie the option to eat here or anywhere she wanted really in the house. Hallie looked up confused, "what do you mean, anywhere?"

"Anywhere, have a garden, balcony, the office, the kitchen, here. You decide."

"Balcony, that sounds, nice. Fresh air might help."

"Follow me." Seb leads the way into another bedroom which Hallie assumed was Seb's bedroom, it was huge, a large bed which was neatly made and large by folded doors on the right-hand side which opened to a beautiful balcony. A metal table and chairs already there and what looked like would be a perfect date scenery. This meal however was not a date just a nice meal with her kidnapper.

The evening was beautiful and peaceful, Hallie was enjoying the fresh warm air whilst she was eating her Chow Mein. Taking in the beautiful gardens it officially didn't feel like she was being held hostage, she was comfortable here. Why was the biggest question. How could she ever trust Seb or anyone ever.

"Ask me."

"What?" Hallie was startled by Seb she didn't understand what he meant and looked over to him not realising she had sauce on her cheek.

Seb wiped the sauce from Hallie's cheek and licked his finger, "ask me what you want."

"The memory stick found in Alex; did you know about it?"

"Yes, he told me he swallowed it before I drugged him, thought I would leave it to you to find." Seb not fazed by anything he continued to eat; he knew more questions like this would come up. The more time he could spend with Hallie the better.

"The diary? The diary found in Parker's desk. It was..."

"Your mothers, yes."

"Why the circled words?"

"Clues for you to find me well now for them to try to find me. They still haven't cracked that code."

"What do you plan on doing once you have dealt with what you want to deal with." Hallie couldn't say the words, Fowler's name made Hallie's body fill with anger, so she chose not to say it.

"You to stay here for as long as you need to, to work with me. To learn that what I do, I do for good. Just, you Hallie."

"You said my name." Hallie put her fork down in shock, he only ever used nicknames for Hallie. He never called her by her name.

"Because I mean it, no jokes. I will show you, give you anything you ever wanted. Treat you how you deserve to be treated, beg, plea, I would kill for you."

41

Gibb entered Fowler's office which to his surprise was not how he left it. There were folders over the floor, papers scattered everywhere, and Fowler sat on Hallie's desk going through her laptop.

"You good?" Gibb knew this was a stupid question, but he needed to say something as Fowler still didn't realise he was stood there.

"Huh, oh yeah, I will clean this up, just needed to let off some steam." Fowler remained calm as if the last few hours had never happened.

"Well, I got us both coffees, you need to go home and get some rest at some point. But me telling you that is like hitting my head against a brick wall so thought we would need this." Gibb handed over the coffee and sat on the other desk to look over the evidence in front of him. To which something sparked up Gibb's interest, he grabbed to paper and began to type.

"What you got?" Fowler stood up and walked over to Gibb, looking over his shoulder to see what he was doing Gibb suddenly stopped.

"The butterfly manor, there is an underground bunker. They had it in the war, was that checked?" Gibb realised that Fowler was already grabbing his coat, he soon followed.

The butterfly manor was still cornered off from the police, Fowler went in with Gibb following close by. This manor was checked by multiple people for any clues, signs of life just how did they miss that it had a bunker. That would be the perfect place for Hallie to be hidden, no one knew except now Fowler and Gibb.

"Should we call for back up?" Gibb went to get his phone out when Fowler stopped him,

"Only if we find something that either doesn't add up right or we find Hallie. Understand?"

"Sure." Gibb was confused, why did Fowler not want to call this in, to explain to Sergeant that this was missed by multiple people, and they may have a lead. Ignoring what Fowler just told him, Gibb sent a location message to Sergeant just to be on the safe side.

As they walk through the abandoned manor, the bunker lay on the side which fortunately hasn't been burnt down. There was a cupboard door at the end of the hallway which led to the stairs down into the basement. The basement was cold, all concrete base and empty. No furniture, no remains just a plain concrete pad. As they walked through the basement, they finally came across a door which was the entrance to the bunker. Fowler had a smile lift across his face, finally he was one step ahead of this freak. A long dark corridor followed from this; it was like a maze this place. Fowler was determined to find out where this ended up. Looking over to Gibb and getting him to turn his torch on his phone also so lighting would be better. Until they were about ten steps in when the door closed suddenly behind them. Instantly they both ran back to the door to try and open it, no luck it was locked.

"There must be another way out, quicker we get there the better." Fowler began walking down the echoed hallway. His footsteps were the only sound you could hear. Finally reaching a metal gate which had a padlock on it. The padlock had numbers which you needed a unique code to open with. Fowler tried Hallie's birthday, one two three four, all zeros, nothing.

"Wait, there was a code used before. In that video, could it be that?"

"Gibb you are brilliant. Fuck what was it?" Fowler was scanning through his camera roll on his phone to which he always had photos of the evidence on him.

"7640."

Sliding the numbers to match this code, the padlock unlocked. "How the fuck did you remember that?"

"I have an eidetic memory."

"Well, after this you need a big promotion and a raise."

"And probably therapy depending on how this turns out." Gibb tried to make it sound like a joke but from what happened on their last trip out he wasn't ruling anything out. From this gate opening, lead them to a large room, it looked like the one Hallie was in from the video. Until everything went black. Gibb was on the floor knocked out. Fowler dropped his phone and went to swing at the figure who tried to hit him. The figure hid back into the shadows to which Fowler tried to follow, another long corridor awaits and he could hear footsteps in the distance. He pulled out a knife not realising he had left Gibb behind, unconscious. A bag was pulled over Fowler's head, his arms began to swing around trying to get it off to he could breathe, attempting to hit the figure which stood behind him. A sharp prick was hit on the side of his neck, he was drugged. Now he lay on the floor cold, unable to move but before he fell into a deep sleep, he saw the figure roll his hood down, crouching down to Fowler close to his face. "Remember this face, because it will be the last one you will ever see." From that Fowler's eyes slowly close and he is out cold.

"Sir, we found a basement door, there is another door down there but is locked."

"Well get it unlocked then."

"Yes sir, we are awaiting the team who can do this."

All Sergeant was thinking was why did Fowler not call this in, call for back up and why did Gibb send the location and nothing else. It didn't add up but now he had three missing people, and this was a shit situation for him to be in.

42

After a shitty past few hours, this evening was so amazing for Hallie. Still sitting on the balcony just staring into the views of the fields, forest, and the beautiful sunset. The sky was clear and was a deep orange with hints of red throughout. The sun was slowly beginning to lower itself behind the trees. Seb came back out with a blanket and draped it over Hallie's shoulders. It wasn't too cold yet but as soon as that sun would set the evening draws closer and it would begin to get colder. Seb took his seat and slid a beer over to Hallie, unsure whether she would take it the offer was nice in her eyes. Without looking at what it was or if he had poisoned it just without thinking Hallie took the beer and placed the cold bottle to her lips and took a couple swigs of it before placing it back on the table.

"Thank you."

Seb wanted to make a comment, wonder if she would make a joke saying he had poisoned it or if he was trying to get her drunk to take advantage. But he held his tongue and just half smiled back to Hallie. He had no words, and after everything he had been up to recently, he had barely slept, this was the first rest he had in what seemed like forever.

"Tell me something about you. Something no one knows." Still no eye contact from Hallie, her eyes still felt slightly puffy from her breakdown earlier.

"Like what?"

"Anything. You know about my whole life, not by my choice but least you make a good stalker remembering everything." Seb let out a small chuckle from this comment. "Just, something, you are a closed book."

Seb cleared his throat and sat up slightly from his chair, he admired the outdoors, nature, and its beauty. He had someone to keep him company in his lonely life and she didn't seem to mind his company.

"Okay, urm well my life I won't lie has been pretty shitty so can't really describe something that has happened that makes you feel better."

"Least we have that in common." Hallie took another two swigs from her beer and this time cradled it to her chest. Pulling her legs up so she could wrap herself in the blanket and face Seb. She was good at getting answers from people, it was part of her job but this time she felt like this was going to be her hardest interrogation ever.

"I don't usually talk about me. So, this is very, weird in my eyes."

"Okay then let me help you, what is your biggest issue you would want to just happen or let it go away."

"Trust. My ability to trust anyone. I just don't, I have been knocked back too many times from trusting the wrong people. It is why I don't talk about my life, I do my job, go home then do it again." Seb didn't look at Hallie when he said this, he was still admiring the sun setting behind the trees. A soft warm glow was shining on both Hallie and Seb and Hallie could see his scar across his cheek which fell down his neck much more clearly. His skin was so clear, had a short stubble beard which was well groomed, and his eyes didn't look dark, they had a flicker of light brown shoot through which brightened his face. Hallie didn't know how to take this; she had met someone who was so similar to her and was slowly forgetting about the past she had with him.

"I agree." Hallie was shocked by Seb's response; she didn't expect him to open up like that so quickly.

"I don't expect you to trust me anytime soon darl, but one day I hope you can. The short time you have been here is probably the most I have ever spoken about myself to anyone."

"I know" Hallie looked back at the sunset to which Seb looked over and stared at her. Hallie could feel his eyes on her but chose to keep looking away, these past few days have been a lot for Hallie to take in and right now she felt like she had no problems going on in her life. She was alone, with nature and it was beautiful.

The sun had finally set, the moon began to shine brightly and low in the sky, all the wildlife sounds changed as nightlife had begun. Hallie still sat wrapped in the blanket however when she looked over, she saw that Seb had his head resting in his hand, eyes closed. He looked, peaceful. Hallie quietly moved her chair close to his, unwrapping the blanket she had around her and gently placed half over Seb and half over herself so that they could both stay warm. Seb didn't move a muscle, so Hallie knew he was asleep, even when his arm twitched that didn't wake him. Hallie didn't want to go in, not yet anyways so she enjoyed the evening views and for once her mind had stopped. Like she was underwater again, everything still, peaceful and nothing to scare her. A gust of wind blew towards them both and through the patio door which had made the curtains move. This however cause one of Seb's aftershave bottles to be knocked over and fall to the floor and smash. This made both Seb and Hallie jump, however Seb's reaction was to grab Hallie and cover her from any danger. Once he had realised what it was, he slowly released Hallie from his grip.

"Sorry."

"It's okay, made me jump too."

"What's with the blanket?" Seb looked down in confusion as he remembers sitting across from Hallie and now she was next to him sharing a blanket.

"It was getting cold, just didn't want you getting cold. Thats all."

"But you are barely covered from it?"

"That's okay, you look like you needed the rest so didn't want to wake you."

"Nope." Seb moved the blanket back over Hallie to make sure she stayed warm, but Hallie was just as stubborn and put it back over him, making her laugh which was a nice sight for Seb.

"Do you not like sharing?" Hallie looked over to Seb still laughing as they put the blanket back and forth.

"I do, but I prefer to do anything to make you, well happy."

"Sharing makes me happy, so take the bloody blanket." Still tossing it back and forth Seb then gets up, picks Hallie up and places her on his lap. Moving the blanket over them both and not making eye contact with her but looking at the moon.

"There, now we both get all the blanket."

Hallie didn't say a word, she didn't even move to get back up. She enjoyed his warmth, his smell, and the view. After everything she had endured from today, this was peace. Seb was almost certain she wouldn't stay like this and would get back up or leave, but to his surprise she didn't. Hallie pointed out the bats which circled right over their heads to which Seb attempted a joke about vampires and if they were real and turned into bats where did their clothes go. This eases any tension between them both. This was all Seb wanted, and he knew he had to show Hallie who he had tied up in his basement sooner or later. But tonight wasn't the night, he wanted to enjoy this moment. Who knew what Hallie's reaction would be when Seb tells her what he has done.

43

Their evening together was perfect, Hallie had fallen asleep in Seb's arms on the balcony, he carried her back to her bed, tucked her in and gently kissed her head. Seb kept her door slightly open, so she didn't feel trapped before ensuring the other doors remained locked. One of the bedrooms, his office, and the basement. Seb headed towards the basement door, locking it behind himself before slowly walking down the concrete steps.

This was it; this was the moment Seb had waited for all these years. Finally, Adam Fowler was in tied up, in his basement ready to receive the worst possible revenge Seb had ever endured. Most of the killings Seb has committed have been for business, for clients but this, this was personal, and he was going to enjoy every bit of it.

Fowler was still unconscious from the drug injected into his neck however, he will wake up in pain from Seb cracking a few of his ribs. He was tied up, very similar to how Hallie was all those years ago, his head hung low blood dripped from is nose. He made a good punch bag for Seb and was nicer that he didn't talk. Seb knew that he would be out for a long time, so he went back upstairs to check on Hallie.

Peering through the gap in the door, Seb tried to be quiet when checking in on Hallie but the floorboard gave him away. Hallie's eyes opened to see Seb looking over at her.

"See your creepy tendencies are still there." Hallie began to sit up in bed when a sharp pain hit her head. Instantly she grabbed her head which Seb came straight over to check her. He had a look of care, compassion and when Hallie looked back up their eyes finally locked with each other. "My head, think I just sat up too quick."

Seb grabbed her with both hands either side of her face and tilted her head down so he could look at the wound to her head and re check the stitches. Hallie was healing but he knew she would still be healing on the inside. "Stitches look good, let me get you some pain meds, might help."

"Honestly, I think was just a little head rush."

"This was my fault; I never should have laid a finger on her." Seb whispered to himself as he left the room and went into his office. Hallie was unsure what to make of this, he seemed sorry. Hallie was slowly seeing another side to this man, he seemed hurt, had regrets, he opened to Hallie and whether she liked it or not her feelings for him changed. He was still a prick for the stuff he done but seeing this side of him was helping Hallie understand him better.

Seb enters the room again with a glass of water and some pain medication for Hallie, placing them on the bedside table for Hallie. Joining her, he placed himself on the edge of the bed. Rest was what he needed, but he made sure Hallie was okay before that.

"You look like shit." Popping the medications in her mouth and taking them with one sip of water.

"Thanks."

"Do you ever sleep?"

"Not really."

"You slept outside with me?"

"No idea how, must have needed it."

"Lay down." Hallie looked at Seb and saw the confusion in his face. He had no idea where she was going with this if she was even being serious.

"Do it, lay down." Hallie held his shoulders and guided him to lay where she was laying before. Seb gave in, he was shattered and could do with the rest. Hallie laid by his side and covered them both with the duvet, she faced towards him and closed her eyes. Hoping that he would do the same Hallie assumed that Seb would fall asleep. Instead, he stared at her, admiring every quality she has, the small cluster of faint freckles which spread over her nose, her long natural black eyelashes which curled so perfectly people would pay money to have them, her hair looked so soft, a few strands cover her face which Seb tucked behind her ears.

"You know to sleep you need to close your eyes." Hallie's eyes still closed but a smile across her face made Seb like her even more. Seb tilted his head back to nest into the pillow and allowed himself to drift off to a sleep. He was a light sleeper if anything was to happen, he would know.

Hallie woke in the middle of the night from another nightmare, but unlike the one she always had, the person beating her was Fowler. He was the one who held everything, who hurt her so badly. Hallie woke up in sweats, her head was pounding again like she was being hit multiple times. Finally catching her breathe she looks over to see that Seb is next to her, not hugging her, not even laying a hand on her just watching.

"Here, have some water." As he handed her the glass, he saw her hands were still shaking. Guilt ran through his body, thinking this was because of him.

"Sorry, had nightmares since I was a kid."

"I did too."

"Did?"

"Rarely sleep long enough for a dream or nightmare to happen now."

"Oh."

"What is it about."

"It used to be the same nightmare, all the time but now it is him. It is Fowler's face; he is the one hurting me. Just, fuck knows. What time is it?"

"2am. Is there anything I can do?" Seb didn't know if it was space or company she needed. Knowing she needed the rest as tomorrow will be the day decisions will need to be made.

"I'm okay, did you sleep at all."

"A bit."

"Then we have some more hours of sleep in store I think." Hallie grabbed the duvet again and laid back down. Seb joined but unsure if he would be able to fall asleep. An hour had past, and he was still awake, thinking how to plan what is to come when he felt warmth on his chest. Hallie had rested her head and cuddled into Seb; he moved his arm to warp around her.

As the morning closed in Seb woke to see Hallie in the same position she was in before he fell asleep. Not wanting to move he lay there contemplating telling her who he had in the house. Hoping she wouldn't see him differently, he had to plan this just right, say the right things. Seb had told Hallie his intentions, and hoping her mind would be changed and viewed Fowler different, this was something he had to do. Hallie woke and looked up at Seb she didn't say anything just smiled and rested her head back on his chest.

"Did you sleep at all?"

Seb began stroking Hallie's hair "I did."

"So, what is going through your head right now to make your face look like that?"

"Lots of things."

"Do you want to talk about it?"

"I will, eventually." Seb still stroking her hair which Hallie didn't seem to mind. She grew fond of Seb's company which was a surprise to her.

Hallie looked up to Seb straight in his eyes which cause him to stop moving, "how about I make us breakfast and can talk about what is going on in your head?" Hallie began to get up when Seb pulled her back into bed.

"I can make us something."

"Then let me help you at least?"

"Okay." Leading her way to the kitchen she knew what she wanted for breakfast which to her surprise Seb was already beginning to make. Fry up was one of Hallie's favourite breakfasts and finally having a big enough appetite for this helped. As Seb dished up all the food to one plate Hallie couldn't help noticing he still had the same facial expression on his face.

"What is it? Sleep make you even more pissed off?" Hallie bit into her hash brown and looked back over to Seb who was buttering the toast. "Talk to me? What's going on?"

"I just, after today I don't want you to think different of me, but I need to show you something." Seb was finally eating and looking over at Hallie, scanning her facial expression to try get some sort of read from it.

"Okay, want to give me the heads up as to what you want to show me?" nothing really fazed Hallie anymore but what she was going to see, who knew how she would take it.

"Not really, no. I have liked these past couple days, I just."

"I know you have my best intentions at heart Seb, you just took a very fucked up route to show it." Hallie smiled and continued to eat. This was also the first time she had called Seb by his real name and not Prick. Seb noticed this and knew what he was going to show her needed to happen sooner rather than later. No lies, no hiding anything just the truth.

"Darl, you know I said I struggle with trusting people. I know you do as well?"

"Yes, but we both have our reasons for that."

"We do yes." Seb paused for a moment and allowed Hallie to finish her orange juice before continuing. "I think might be better for me to show you."

Hallie stood up and followed Seb to his bedroom, unsure of what was going on he handed her a black hoodie which covered her up. It wasn't cold outside, but Hallie still took it and put it on. They headed over to one of the rooms which had been locked since Hallie got here.

"If there is a dead person in here, I will be pissed off."

"I can assure you, there are no dead bodies in this house."

"So, what is with the hoodie."

"To keep you warm. Darl, before I let you in just know I have not harmed this person in any way, in fact he is the one person on your crappy team I would hire for myself."

"Right, what's the point here?"

"Just, thought you would want to have a conversation with him, he is the one who has shown all your team the corrupt videos of Fowler. Just hear each other out." As Seb said this, he placed his arm around Hallie, unlocked the door and stepped in the room with her. Hallie was in shock to see a familiar face So much she needed to tell them, but not realising what she was about to hear.

"Gibb?"

44

Hallie was in shock to see Gibb sat on the bed. This bedroom was smaller than Hallie's however still well decorated. It had an en-suite no shower or bath just toilet and sink so least Hallie had the luxury. Gibb was accompanied by the same doctor who done Hallie's stitches on her head which looked like Gibb was receiving the same treatment.

"Hallie! Are you, ow ow okay need to stop moving. Are you okay?" Gibb tried to get up not realising the doctor was still stitching his head.

Hallie looked up to Seb, "No harm hey, what's with the stitches."

"Was either that or drug but couldn't grab him in time. Smaller cut than yours though."

"Hallie, my dear you are looking well. Better than last time we saw each other. He only needs a couple stitches, was fine when he came in just irritated it in his sleep looks like."

"I'm sorry, you all know each other?" Gibb looked around confused at the situation. "Hallie, I thought you was being, tortured, beaten, well kidnapped been trying to find you?"

"Doc, think we need to leave these two in peace." Seb encouraged the doctor to leave so that Gibb and Hallie could talk alone. "I'll be around if you need me, okay?" Seb looked down to Hallie wanting to just hug her, touch her, but thought best to give her time and space.

"Thank you." The door closed and Hallie went to join Gibb on the bed.

"Hal, I'm sorry but I'm very fucking confused right now?"

"You and me both."

"Is that the person who took you?"

"Yes."

"And you two are what, buddies now."

"When you learn all the information, I slowly understood the reasons behind it all?"

"Didn't he hurt you."

"Well, he hit the back of my head and knocked me out yes, but he regretted that as was going to drug me so didn't feel a thing, but I woke up in the night and well guess you know the rest. But yes, he was the one who tortured me in Afghanistan but again need to learn the reasons why." Before Hallie could continue Gibb jumped in.

"Fowler."

"What do you know?"

"I know I can't trust him now. I used to until I saw the footage of him killing that person who was his teammate and shooting him."

"Gibb, that was his brother. Sebastian's brother was the person Adam shot and killed and tried killing Seb too."

"And he wouldn't let me call for back up when we got to the manor before I ended up here."

"What, why?"

"Said no point calling for it unless we found you or something worth calling for?"

"Fuck sake."

"I still did anyway so they probably hunting for us now."

"Most likely, what else do you know."

"I know that Sergeant and your old boss in the army gave him a rough time and threatened his job for all the mistakes he made."

"Gibb, I am going to tell you some things now and I need your honest opinion please."

Gibb looked at Hallie and got himself comfortable on the bed. "Okay, what?"

"I also have learned that Fowler was the one who held me back from getting onto special forces. Our commanding officer on that mission where he killed Seb's brother didn't know about it until my extraction mission. He also shot at the commanding officer who happened to be like a brother to me and he died on route to the hospital. Harris, his name was. Fowler carried us both out to make him look like the war hero. He also went for my job but when I got accepted, he took the role below me so we could work together. The reason I was tortured all those years ago by Seb is because he thought I was working with Adam and took revenge this way."

"Fuck! That is fucked up Hallie."

"Tell me about it."

"So, what is this place? And who is this person who has taken us."

"This, well I think it is Seb's house, he runs his own business as such, eliminating bad people."

"So, a murderer?"

"In some ways, yes. But they have to have a pretty fucked up reason for why they get under Seb's radar to be killed by him and his team."

Gibb had a look of even more confusion across his face. "So, your okay with this, and him?"

"I wasn't, I guess I am. I don't know. This is a fucked up situation."

"Your telling me."

"Why was you out of the office anyways Gibb?"

"Went with Fowler to follow the lead that you were in the abandoned manor, the dick left me to die when was knocked out."

"What?"

"I was hit but still conscious, and Fowler just looked at me and then carried on going."

Hallie looked around the room, this was setting stone, Gibb who was just a tech guy saw firsthand that Fowler wasn't in it for the team but for himself. Seb knocked the door before letting himself in, Hallie smiled at his entrance but Gibb still unsure.

"So, you are the guy that has been hacking in every system and over-riding everything?" Gibb asked with a shake in his voice, he wanted to learn hacking so badly but didn't know where he stood with Seb.

"I am. I can teach you if you like. I am impressed with your level of skills too." Seb showed little emotion, but Hallie noticed Gibb still looking uneasy at the whole situation. "Gibb, I would hire you to work for me if you ever wanted to. Police work is limited, here you have everything. Think on it. I would like to show you something, if you'll let me, as an apology for making you need stitches." Hallie stood up and smiled at Seb mouthing the words Thank you.

"Uhh, yeah. Sure." Gibb followed and Hallie knew exactly where Seb was taking them both. However, in his office was someone she had never met before. A young woman, early twenties, bright blonde hair and piercing blue eyes. Glasses which nearly cover her whole face.

"Kat, sorry Katie, I would like you to meet…" Before Seb could finish his sentence, Katie was already on her feet and walking towards Hallie to shake her hand.

"Hallie Jones, have heard loads about you, finally amazing to put the name to the face. And you..." Katie stopped and looked Gibb up and down and smiled.

"This is Gibb Katie. Katie, Gibb. Katie is one of our top hackers, recruited her when she was in high school. Favor from her parents. Katie, would you mind showing Gibb what you're up to for a while?"

"Happily." Katie grabbed Gibb's hand and pulled him to the desk; this was like his heaven. So many monitors, coding, cameras footage. He would be happy there plus working with someone his age and who was good looking was a bonus.

"You going to be alright in here Gibb." Hallie looked over and it was like sending her kid off to play toys which made her laugh.

"Oh yes, I will be great, long as no one here is going to kill me?" Gibb looks over to Seb who is shaking his head.

"No. No one is here to kill you, help yourself to anything in the kitchen if you guys get hungry, Katie knows where everything lives. Just, Katie start off easy with the hacking, like police data base or something."

Hallie left Gibb to his own devices. Laughing away at how happy he was made her feel comfort. "Where did you find him?" Hallie looked over to Seb who was walking next to her.

"At the trail I had left for your team so they could find you. Gibb was the only one with common knowledge and was able to track you down."

"Really?"

"Yes. He was abandoned though and left to fend for himself, so I grabbed him and brought him here." Seb placed his hand around Hallie's waist to guide her back to the kitchen so they could get a drink.

"So, where is Fowler?" this name still made Seb so angry, but he kept his composure in well.

"I don't think you're ready for that yet?"

"How would you know?"

"Because I don't want to lose you and he is going to pay for what he has done not only to you but to others."

"What do you mean others?" Hallie held a cup of tea in her hands and Seb was hesitant to tell her this next bit of information.

"Okay, before I tell you, that boiling hot cup of tea you are holding, that stays in the mug and not thrown anywhere. Got it?"

"Fine."

"Fowler didn't have a close family, I mean he had family but they all re located to Australia when he came back from the army, his house wasn't bought as a congratulations for getting the job it was his dads house which he rented as they lived away. He also had got someone pregnant." That was it, Hallie put the tea on the table and both hands in her head.

"What!"

"Yes, her name is Arabella, she is now 3 years old, he still has a relationship with her and the mother."

"He has a fucking family!"

"Yes."

"You are taking the piss."

"No, the mother of the kid still believes they are together, and he just works long distance."

"So, he had been fucking me when he had a family elsewhere?" Hallie was so angry right now; this was the tip off the edge she didn't need. Full of hate and anger she needed to let off some steam.

"Hallie, he is here. But I can't let you see him, not yet."

"Why, is he dead?"

"No, but not awake yet, when he is you can release as much anger you have okay?"

"He'll be dead by the time I'm done with him I'm telling you that. Fuck!" Hallie got up off her chair and began to pace. This was emotional pain, betrayal by someone she thought she could trust. How could she have missed that?

"Seb?"

"Yes darl?" his eyes were still mesmerizing; she knew what she wanted and him going to all these lengths just for her proves that. Hallie walks over to Seb and places both her hands on his face and kisses him. Seb grabs hold around her waist and pulls her into the kiss. Seb had waited for this moment for years, he didn't care if it was through anger, sadness, anything it was still perfect. Seb grabbed

Hallie around her waist and lifted her onto the breakfast bar, her legs wrapping around his body to which they were interrupted.

"Woah?" Gibb and Katie were in the doorway which was not helpful. "Well, Katie was just uh, showing me around. Can come back?"

"No, it's uh fine. I'll be back." Hallie looked at Seb to which he followed her out with his eyes. Which then lead to looking at Gibb.

"Smooth." Both Katie and Gibb said at the same time then started to laugh.

Seb left the room to follow Hallie upstairs. She was not in her room though but back on the balcony looking over the views. Seb came in and hugged her from behind resting his chin on her shoulder.

"I don't want to rush you darl."

"You're not, I wanted that to happen. And will happily let it happen again." Hallie moved her head to rest against Seb.

"In couple hours, he will be awake and can give him a taste of his own medicine. Okay."

"Bring it on."

45

Never in a million years would Hallie have thought she would be in this situation. From being one of the top people in her division at work, working case by case and thinking she was finally happy. To being taken by the person who tortured her 10 years ago, learning that the person she thought she could trust more than anyone else in the world lived in a world of endless lies, and the person who she thought she hated more than anyone else that ever lived she had just kissed and agreed to let Adam Fowler get what he deserved. How quickly times change. Gibb was now also being held at the same manor Hallie was however, unlike Hallie who in the beginning resented from being there this place was like a field day for Gibb, endless amounts of technology to play with and use, learning things he has wanted to pursue. Safe to say it took Gibb less time to adjust to life here than it did for Hallie.

The evening was drawing in and Seb had ordered dinner for everyone, Hallie did wonder where all his money came from as living in a place like this, having a collection of cars, the technology everywhere must have cost him a fortune. Realising Seb was a caring person as he has allowed all these people to be in his house and had supplied everything. Katie had brought in clothes in for Hallie, she had broken into Fowler's house and stole some of her clothes. Hallie was grateful for this however seeing her old clothes made her want to burn them all. They had been in his house, or what she thought was his house. The sooner she got to talk to Fowler and find out why the hell he did this to her the better.

"Hey, just checking in." Gibb quietly knocked the door and entered Hallie's room where she still was in Seb's clothes and staring at her own. "Taken to wearing comfy now, have you?" Gibb let out a chuckle which Hallie smiled along however Gibb knew something else was going on.

"I want to just burn it all." Hallie picked up the black bag with all her old work clothes I and put them in the cupboard.

"Why? They are your clothes, right?"

"Yes, but they just remind me of all those years I have worn the same look, same style and reminds me of that prick."

Gibb joined Hallie sitting on the edge of the bed, "Do you think you'll go back?"

"What to work, at the moment I don't want to."

"What so leave the police?" Gibb seemed shock at this response, Hallie's life was her job and had no idea she had been thinking this.

"Yeah, I don't want to go back, I can't go back. I could do anything really. Just, the thought of working back there now makes me feel sick. I lived in a lie, I trusted him Gibb and I don't trust anyone, but I opened up to someone who has another life, a family a..."

"A what!" Gibb interrupted, apparently this bit of information was left out to Gibb.

"He has a kid, and the mother of the kid believes they are still together, but he works long distance as a cop."

"Fuck. Off."

"Wish I was lying."

"What a slimy prick. No wonder you are feeling like this. Can I ask you something?"

"Sure?"

"That kiss back in the kitchen, that looked real. Your mind must be so confused?"

"It was, but surprisingly my mind is clear. No confusion."

"But didn't he, you know".

"Yes, but a very long time ago. But I don't see him like that, not anymore."

"Have you both, you know..."

"No, that was the first proper moment I have had with him. We spent an evening together but no is the answer to your question."

"Not yet then hey" Gibb nudged Hallie with his elbow and began to laugh. He was good at easing the tension and it was nice for Hallie to have someone who she knew well enough to talk to.

"If Seb offered you a job, would you take it."

"Yes" Gibb didn't even think about it. He wanted to stay and work here; this was something he had always wanted to pursue but police work was the safe option.

"Don't blame you, you look like a kid in a candy shop."

"I am. That office, is the definition of porn in my eyes."

"Well, your porn is a lot different to mine Gibb." That was it, laughter emerged from them both, this was what Hallie needed. Unaware that Seb was outside and had heard most of that conversation he finally knocked the door and made them both aware that he had dinner downstairs.

Gibb went ahead hoping Katie was still here which to his delight she was already eating her burger. Seb and Hallie held back and slowly walked together. "Preferring my clothes, are you?"

"I am, I want to burn all my old clothes and start fresh I think."

"Okay, after you've eaten grab my laptop and order whatever you want. Katie knows a clothing brand which delivers next day so order tonight and would be here in the morning."

"No brand I have ever known does that, beside if I use my card to pay for it, they could track that and find me that way."

"Who said anything about you paying for it?" Seb continued to walk looking straight ahead whilst Hallie looked up to him with gratitude shining through.

"When they have stopped looking for me, I will pay you back."

"Deal."

"I think I need to go and see Sergeant." This was what made Seb stop and look at Hallie.

"Why?"

"So, they know I am okay, and to stop looking for me."

"And so, you can go back?"

"No, I will be resigning." Hallie didn't make a decision before, but the words had already left her mouth and she knew this was the right thing to do.

"And do what?"

"No idea. I will have a break from everything, then decide I think."

"Could work with me?" Seb began walking again but Hallie stayed still then realising he was not stopping; she began to try and catch up to him.

"Say that again."

"You have training, you would be good. Obviously take your break first then can work with me." Hallie began to realise he had said with him not for him. Like a partner maybe. "You have time to think on it. Need to get some food in you, this evening isn't going to be an easy one for you." Seb pulled her into his body and kissed her forehead before heading into the kitchen and taking a seat. Conversations were flowing, laughing, and feeling the most normal, not a trap and like a home. Katie was helping Hallie order a whole new wardrobe whilst Seb gave Gibb a new laptop and was showing him some new tricks.

Seb gave Katie a nod to which she said to Gibb that she would show him around the house, and she had to hack into a database for a job coming up if he wanted to help. Gibb didn't shy away from this opportunity and gladly left with Katie. Which left Hallie and Seb alone in the kitchen, once again.

"You did the nod."

"You noticed that?"

"I use that nod; I know what it means."

"You sure you want to talk to him?"

"Yes, I want the truth to leave his mouth."

"Okay. It isn't nice down there, okay. Most, business, is conducted down there."

"I'm sure I have seen worse. I will be fine." Hallie had no idea what to expect when Seb took her down the basement. But when she reached the bottom step and the beam light came on, she knew that was not what she was expecting.

46

This was it, the waiting, the agony that Seb had been feeling for so long was finally coming closer. Hallie still was unsure on what Seb was planning on doing to Fowler and at this rate that was the last thing on her mind now. Hallie wanted the truth to come out of his mouth, to find out why he had done this to her and why after all these years he did not tell her the truth about what really happened in Afghanistan. Seb placed his arm around Hallie and gave her a reassuring look, "I'll be over their if you need me okay."

Hallie stepped into the light for Fowler to be able to see her. Shock appeared over his face, as he wondered why she was standing in front of him. He had a black eye, busted lip, must have multiple internal injuries however for the first time ever, Hallie felt sick and nervous around Fowler.

"Hallie, are you okay? What's going on?" Fowler began to struggle however his chains kept him bounded. Curling over in pain he tried to fight through it but stopped moving completely when the pain got too much.

"I have one main question. Why did you lie?" Hallie kept calm and collected, she stood tall and had her arms crossed, Seb was sat in the dark corner so Fowler would believe that they were both alone.

"What? Lie, what are you talking about? Hal, are you okay, get me out of here have been everywhere trying to find you. Did he hurt you?"

"Stop. Just stop talking. Answer my question with a real answer and not some excuse or another question. I need answers."

"To what, I have no idea what you are talking about?" Fowler began to struggle in the chains again.

"I wanted to give you the opportunity to be open with me. Must live in your web of lies so deeply you forget. Okay let's change the question, would your daughter miss you if you were dead?"

Silence. You could hear a pin drop in the room. Hallie remained tall and was looking Fowler directly in the eye. From having no response from Fowler Hallie continued to talk for him until he cracked.

"Oh, come on Adam, you know how we deal with the silent treatment at work, why give it to me now? Let me tell you the web of lies you have led me to believe shall we start right at the beginning when you put a bad word in for my papers to be accepted to enter special forces." Fowler's head was now hanging low. "Or was it when you said I wouldn't be good enough for this department and I don't belong there. Maybe when Harris stood up for me, that too a bit of your pride did it? So why did you shoot Harris then?" Fowlers' head shot up, looked Hallie directly in the eye and attempted to lie again by stuttering. "How do you- "

"You see it doesn't matter how I know; it is that I know. You also have a secret life and another family; your parents don't even live in the country for fuck sake. You have a long-distance relationship with your baby mumma but still had sex with me. What's that about?"

"Hallie, please"

"Oh, now you beg for forgiveness. Why?"

"She is only young. Please tell me he hasn't harmed them?"

Hallie couldn't answer this as she had no idea what Seb would have them or if he had done anything to them.

"Why did you lie to me Adam?"

"I, I didn't realise I was going to fall for you this much, I was going to end it with her I swear but couldn't do it until I went back to see them in person."

"So, you decided to fuck me before ending it with her?"

No answer, Fowler was speechless, this was not what he thought was going to happen.

"You fucking disgust me, and you deserve everything you have coming for you."

"Answer me this then Hallie, why do you trust that son of a bitch so much huh!"

"Because in the short time I have known him he has told me more truths than you ever have in 10 fucking years!" Voices were being raised and Hallie lost her calm composure and was now in Fowler's face.

"You just wanted to fuck him didn't you. You absolute sl- ". Before he could finish Hallie had head butted Fowler which caused his nose to start bleeding.

"Don't you fucking dare call me that. You have no idea what is going on and honestly you can't talk. You don't deserve any shed of happiness."

"So how do you plan on getting away with it. They will realise I am missing, try to find me. You will be spotted sooner or later and then what Hallie. You going to help him kill me?"

"I will enjoy hurting you like you have hurt me." Through gritted teeth she was pressing into his ribs with a fist making Fowler squirm.

"You will let my daughter grow up not knowing who I am? Huh?"

Hallie began to walk away and up the stairs; Seb turned the lights off before punching Fowler in the stomach once again making him scream. Leaving him chained up Seb walked up the stairs to follow Hallie and knowing exactly where she would be.

The evening was beautiful yet again, sun setting and nature showing off its natural beauty. Seb closed the door behind him and grabbed a blanket to drape over Hallie's shoulders. He wasn't sure if it was because she was cold or adrenaline from what had just happened most likely a bit of both. "Sorry, needed a minute." Hallie was leaning over the balcony enjoying the gentle breeze through her hair.

"Take all the time you need darl. Did better than I thought you would if I'm honest." Seb took a seat on the wooden chair and the silhouette of Hallie and the sunset in the distance would make the perfect photo or painting, these thoughts would race through Seb's head. Knowing he had won over Hallie and was able to get her to trust him was an achievement, but it isn't over yet.

"What are you going to do with his kid and family?"

"Nothing. His death would be made to look like a car accident, and they would be none the wiser. Usually, I just make them disappear but I don't have vengeance with them it is with him."

"Okay."

"Do you want me to get rid of them?"

"No, I still don't know how comfortable I feel with you just killing him with ease and faking his death."

"I didn't want anything to come back on you negatively, you have been through enough, so I learnt that you are my priority he is just an infestation that needs to be fumigated." This made Hallie chuckle, she looked over to Seb who was smiling over at her, she moved his arms and placed herself on his lap.

Three sharp knocks on the door startled both Seb and Hallie. Before Hallie could get up Seb picked her up and placed her back in the chair so he could go see who it was. Both Katie and Gibb were at the door and Seb invited them in. "You need to see this." Katie gave Seb the laptop screen and he began to read. Hallie got up and went inside to see what everything was about.

"Can you get me in?"

"Yes, already have two tickets for you, we can hack the security system to watch what is going on and communicate with you on the outside."

"Dates?"

Now Gibb spoke up which surprise Hallie, had he already been appointed and hired. "14th September. Black tie formal."

"Well, that looks around the time you get off your little break from working." Turning to Hallie smiling however she had no idea what he was talking about.

"I'm sorry?"

"From what Seb is saying, looks like you are his date to the masquerade ball."

"A ball, are you serious?"

"Deadly."

"Why a ball?"

"Because our target will be attending and that is where we will be extracting him and getting some answers."

Still confused Hallie just ended up agreeing, who knew what she would be doing in 6 months' time, but it was easier to just say yes then keep asking what was going on. Slowly learning what Seb's job was is still a challenge but hopefully will come with time.

47

Fowler was doing everything he could to escape his chain, any way to get out of this cold dark room and out into the open. Never in a million years would he have thought Hallie would turn on him like this, learn the truth and trust the man he believed she despised. Nothing could have prepared Fowler for this, he had been in some difficult situations before however this was an all-time new for him. Suddenly, he heard the click of the lock on the door at the top of the stairs, instantly he pulls his hands out of the chains, trying to dislocate his thumb, old trick in the book to slip cuffs. However, no matter how hard he pulled it was not budging.

"You can't slip them." Seb's voice had a hint of amusement in watching him struggle, he made a bet with himself that he could make Fowler cry before he died.

"What do you want with me. Okay, I am sorry I killed your partner and shot you and took MY extraction target."

"But he wasn't yours, was he. We all were working together until you and your little teammates turned your back and attempted to kill me, successfully killing my brother."

"I didn't know he was your brother."

"Would it have mattered; you would've done it anyways. You wanted to play the hero, the one who succeeded but until your teammate and commanding officer Harris got a scent of what your game was, well you had to get rid of him too. You are a snake, coward, and a liar."

Fowler had no response; he was unsure how he knew everything even Harris but accepted that there was probably no way out.

"I have changed since then."

"Bull shit. You still lied to Hallie for years, never told her about your child or you having another life. You left your IT guy for dead,"

"Gibb, is he okay?"

"Don't act like you care, you left him. Someone with no training in the field, no policing or military experience to fend for himself. Who does that?" Seb still spoke calmly however it wouldn't take much to make him loose his composure.

"Hallie wouldn't want you to kill me, she works for..."

"I know what she does and how she works. She doesn't care what I do to you, because at least I told her everything, your lies. I had to hurt her emotionally so that she learnt who you truly are. Now, well you saw what she was like to you earlier."

"You were here?"

"Of course, I wouldn't leave her alone with someone as manipulative as you. You are someone I have wanted to hurt for so long. Now you will feel every ounce of pain you have brought on everyone around you."

"They will find you, if you kill me, hurt me, they will find you."

"Worth that risk."

Seb had a smile spread across his face as he pulled out a metal bat from behind his back and swung it around which let out a loud slap onto Fowler's bare chest. Fowler began to scream in agony. Seb dropped the bat and grabbed Fowler by his hair and pulled it his head up whispering in his ear, "I like a fair fight." From this he pressed the large red button which dropped the chains from the ceiling making Fowler drop to the ground. Released finally from the chains Fowler attempted to get up however fell back to the ground several times. Finally finding his feet he was able to stand, not as tall as he used to but still was to his feet.

"I'll let you throw a couple hits in the mix but don't think you will last."

"Please, just let me go."

"Oh begging, not very tough now are you. There are no short cuts in this game, and it will only end one way." Seb removed his top to which both were now bare chested. Fowler saw the scars over Seb's body however was trying to observe his body to try and find a weak spot to take him down with. Then he attempted to run towards Seb and swung for him but swiftly dodged the punch.

Seb allowed one hard punch to his head to make it fair, but this only rattled his cage more. Fowler somehow found the strength to fight back, moving quickly from any fists or kicks coming his way. Seb went in with a sharp hit to Fowler's chest which Fowler then caught his grasp and spun Seb around, getting Seb into a head lock and began tightening his grip with any strength he had remaining. Seb managed to pull Fowler over his head getting himself out the head lock to which Fowler kicked Seb on the right side of his face.

Shaking that off spitting out the blood from his mouth, Seb stood up whilst Fowler attempted to crawl away and from this Seb grabbed both of his feet and dragged him. Trying to get himself off Seb's grip, Fowler began to struggle however was on his belly being dragged so not much help. He tried to grab a hold of anything he could in sight to stop him but missed every time. Seb then let go of his grip causing Fowler's legs to fall letting out a grunt from the pain. Seb kicked him in the head which eventually caused him to be knocked out.

Attaching Fowler back to his chains but instead of having him hoisted back up to be hung he left him on the floor, hoping internal injuries would kill him. Seb could just end his life now, but he wanted Hallie to be safe and free, so this plan seemed to be the best option. Seb turned off the lights and walked to the stairs locking the door behind him. He caught a glimpse of himself in the hallway mirror and decided he would need to get cleaned up before anyone saw him but that was already too late. Seb wasn't expecting anyone to still be awake, but Hallie had emerged from the kitchen with a pint of water. Noticing Seb bare chested and bleeding Hallie placed the glass of water on the dresser in the hallway and walked up to Seb.

"What did you do?" Hallie grabbed hold of Seb's face by the chin and was turning his head for him.

"Nothing."

"Well, that is a good lie right there. Come on." Hallie made Seb follow her to the kitchen as she pulled out a first aid kit which was surprisingly low on supplies but knowing what they do for a living that was expected. Running a cloth under cold water she placed this onto Seb's face. Then taking focus to his mouth which now had a busted lip she got another cloth and put this to his mouth.

"What happened?" Hallie was pressing the cold compress to Seb's face and clearing up any blood he had on him.

"Let him have a few swings, fair fight then."

"Judging by the way you look; sure he looks just as bad."

"Oh worse, but that was expected."

"Did you just feel the need for a fight at one in the morning?"

"Just, will help with the plan. Needed to let some anger out."

"I would recommend a punch bag for future references maybe?" Hallie looked up to him to see him smiling at this comment. Seb headed upstairs to shower before getting into bed to his surprise Hallie was already led in his bed. She had her own room, but Seb was more than happy for her to be with him as was she.

"Can I ask you something?"

"Tomorrow."

"Huh?"

"I know what you were going to ask me."

"Okay, do you want any help?" Seb was shocked by this response; he walked over to the bed and pulled the sheets over himself and allowed Hallie to cuddle into him.

"I couldn't ask you to do that."

"You didn't I offered."

"You need to stay here, no one will ask you questions as we will be making Fowler take wrap for you being 'missing'".

"How do you manage that?"

"You will find out in the morning."

48

Hallie had asked Seb if she could have one final conversation with Fowler before everything. She didn't know if his plan would go well or not but she needed to let this off her chest before. Hallie turned on the lights to see Fowler curled up in a ball and squinting from being in the dark so long his eyes were sensitive to lights. He didn't move much as the pain was too high.

"Back for round two then?"

"Wasn't here to watch round one so can't be that."

"Hallie?"

"Well done dip shit."

"Still pissed at me then?"

"Well, the feelings aren't going to go away just like that are they. Why did you do it?"

"So, I could be the best, the one spoken about. Just, I don't like people to be above me."

"Jealousy. That is it?"

"Yes, I guess it is."

"So why try pursue something with me when you have someone else with a child?" Hallie sat herself on the floor facing Fowler however one thing Fowler didn't realise was that Seb was sat on in the corner making sure he wouldn't try anything.

"Thought could have it all."

"You don't understand how shitty that makes me feel right. I wish I knew who she was so I could tell her what a scumbag, selfish prick you are."

"I am sorry Hallie."

"I don't believe you." Hallie went to stand up when Fowler stood up quickly and grabbed Hallie around the throat in a head lock, Seb stood up suddenly and went to help Hallie and finally finish Fowler off. This was the final straw and his was hurting someone he cared too much about. Fowler was breathless, he was using every bit of last energy and strength he had to keep a hold of Hallie by her throat. He knew that Seb was watching so this seemed a good way to get back at him.

"Go on then Adam, kill me. See where that gets you." Seb stayed hidden in the dark ready to pounce at the right moment. He knew Hallie could handle herself and get out of this but just in case he stayed close enough.

"I'm going to die anyways may as well take you with me."

"Good luck with that. Get your hands off me."

"That isn't what you used to say to me."

"You make me sick; you are a disgusting human being who doesn't deserve the life you have had."

"You used to love it when I was dominating over you Hal, what's changed." Fowler was whispering into Hallie's ear and Seb's blood was beginning to boil he was ready to kill him until Hallie hit him straight in his balls which made him loose his grip around Hallie's neck and fall to his knees. Hallie turned around and kneed him directly in his face causing him to fall closer to the floor.

"That all you got Hal, you used to scream my name, beg for me and-" another knee to the face stopping the words to come out of Fowler's mouth. Kicking him in the ribs multiple times and then to end it with a swift kick to his balls which let out a scream of pain.

"I will never let your name roll off my tongue ever again. You are dead to me and never, never will you touch me, look at me even speak to me. You are a pig, and just to add to your little ego boost," Hallie crouched down to Fowler's head so he could hear this better, "I faked it every time. Must admit you was never that good in bed." Hallie stood back up and walked away heading over to Seb. Fowler looked up to see them both standing together and watched as he kissed her passionately right in front of his eyes.

"Enjoy hell, you peace of shit." Hallie then left the room and headed back up the stairs.

"Any last words?" Seb said with a smile, his hands behind his back.
"Go to hell, you piece of shit."

Seb moved his hands to show Fowler what he was holding a large plastic bag. Walking over to the wall he pushed the red button on the wall which enabled the chains to pull Fowler up and keep him in one position. Seb then grabbed the plastic bag and put it over Fowler's head causing him to suffocate. Fowler began to struggle, his legs swinging every direction you could imagine. Trying to get his hands down so he could pull the bag off his face however Seb's grip was too much, too strong until Fowler's body just stopped, and his head hung down. Seb remained there for a few moments longer just to make sure he was really gone that is when his body began to twitch. Seb moved the bag to one hand keeping it over Fowler's head he checked for a pulse. Nothing. Finally, the man he had wanted dead all these years, was finally dead.

Rain fell in heavy droplets; the sound was mesmerizing like you could drift off to sleep with it. The balcony was covered so you were still able to sit outside without a drop of rain touching you. Hallie was wrapped in a blanket and curled up on the chair listening to the rain fall. Puddles forming on the ground below and the sound of the trees moving in the gentle breeze. Nature truly was magnificent and beautiful no matter how it comes. Hallie closed her eyes for a moment to try and find a point in her mind where she was at peace, her head had been spinning around so much, too many thoughts crossed her mind however now everything seemed clear, straight forward, and positive. Hallie heard the bedroom door open a few moments later however still stayed in the same position and kept her eyes closed. Seb didn't want to startle her, so he went into the bathroom and freshened up before joining Hallie.

Seb took the other seat on the balcony which Hallie didn't like. Getting up she walked over to Seb; he opened his arms out inviting her to sit on his lap. "So, now what?"

"He has been taken to a car wreckage where he will be found there by whoever walks that path. You can meet with your boss tomorrow and explain what happened, who he was and that you had been threatened by him and held captive. Gibb can join you he has already been briefed. Then from there, is up to you darl. To do whatever and go wherever you please."

"There are couple faults to that plan."

"What's that?" Seb knew his plan was thought through and done correctly, there was no faults but was intrigued to know what he has done wrong.

"You said boss, that would be my old boss. I will tell him all of that but adding my resignation in the mix to as I am currently sat on my new boss." A smile was across both of their faces and knowing what was coming next, was words Seb was waiting to hear for a long time.

"And the other fault?"

"Where I please hey? Well, I think I am pretty well pleased here don't you think?"

"I reckon there could be room for improvements, don't you." Seb grabbed the back of Hallie's head however Hallie went in for a kiss Seb stopped it. Confusion was across her face, unsure what was going on she began to move her head back but couldn't move too far as his hand still had a tight grip to Hallie's head.

"You sure you want me, Hallie. I have a lot of shit going on in my life and I want you to be happy?"

"How about you let me decide what I want and don't want hey."

"I just don't want what happened all those years ago to make you hate me?"

"Unfortunately for you, I have already fallen and what happened back then doesn't feel like you. I like this person who is in front of me now, who has my best interests at heart. It is safe to say think we both bring some baggage along with us. But I don't want anyone else. Understand. Now will you shut up and kiss me."

49

'Breaking news just in, a car has been found in a wreckage on the outside of Salisbury Forest. The driver was found dead at the scene and police are treating the scene as not suspicious. Detective Inspector Adam Fowler has been found dead at the scene and has been on police radar for the past week from the disappearance of his partner Detective Inspector Hallie Jones. We have been informed that Detective Fowler had taken his partner and held her in a hostage situation. His story was beginning to unfold and instead of being found out, police believe he tried fleeing leaving his life behind however lost control of the car and crashed into a tree at high-speed causing multiple internal injuries which was cause of death. Police have confirmed that Detective Fowler was also behind the three murders which had taken place this year. Three friends were found separately however all targeted by the same killer. Adam Fowler previously served in the army in special forces before becoming a Detective Inspector with the constabulary. His partner and head inspector of the case Detective Inspector Hallie Jones has since resigned from her position and has given no comment to being taken and held hostage by someone who she considered a work colleague, partner, and friend. It has been said to believe that Hallie was very close to finding out who the killer was to these three victims which was the cause to Adam Fowler taking her hostage so he wouldn't be found out. More to follow on this developing story.'

"Hallie, wait."

"Sir?"

"I understand the resignation, after everything you have been through you deserve a break from it all. Just know if you ever want to return to your position or take another you are always welcome back. I am sorry I didn't notice sooner his behaviour and lies he told and wasn't able to see the harm he caused you."

"Thank you, sir, I will keep your offer in mind however right now I need to keep away from it all and take some time for myself. No one saw the lies he told us sir, and quite frankly I spent so much time with him I don't know how he did it. But it is done now, and I need to move on."

"I understand. If you need me, for anything just give me a call, okay?"

"Yes sir. Thank you again."

Hallie left the building with her cardboard box in her arms, all her belongings from her desk filled this box. It did feel weird for her to be leaving this place, even weirder going back into her office she once shared with Fowler, but this was the right thing to do. A car horn went off which made Hallie turn to the car park to see what was going on and it was Seb in his black Jaguar I-Pace, he had waited for her so she wouldn't have to take a taxi back. Putting her box of belongings in the boot she climbed into the passenger seat and looked over to Seb.

"The world bought it then."

"They sure did."

"How does it feel being out of there?"

"Weird, nice to be out but I spent so much of my life with my work be strange not going back but at the same time I am so happy I don't have to step foot in that building ever again!"

"Good, so anywhere you want to go first for your big break away from working?"

"Home, I think. Book a holiday get away for a few weeks then see where life takes me, I reckon."

"Sounds like a plan darl."

50

6 months later

"You two got a visual?"

"We sure do and must admit you both look like the best-looking couple there is at this event." Gibb and Katie were in the van parked a few streets away which held a whole variety of computer systems, technology, and a satellite so they were able to hack into anything close by.

"Good, did you get into the radio frequency to catch anything there."

"Just come live now Hal, we are ready to go."

"Perfect, Wren you boys in position?"

"Indeed, all snipers in potions and have visuals of the building and inside. May I just add sir that Hallie you look amazing tonight, will have to send a text to the misses showing that you can make an effort." Hallie chuckled and Seb pulled his arm round her closer bending down to whisper in her ear, "You look amazing no matter what you are wearing. Or not wearing."

"Okay, if you guys are going to do sexy talk or anything like that may I remind you this is an open line for us all so we will all hear it."

"What's the matter Gibb, it's like listening to free porn." Wren laughed making this comment whilst watching Seb and Hallie's reaction down the scope of his sniper.

"Well, it might be for you lot but that is like hearing about my sister's sex life. It is weird okay." Katie was laughing at Gibb, his confidence was so much better since he worked for Seb and Katie helped bring his personality out more.

"Eyes on the target, he is sat right side of the bar, sixth person in. How are we going to get him away from his little group. I can cause a distraction so you can swoop in and grab him." Wren was sometimes trigger happy, enjoyed seeing the ones who were not good people suffer.

"How about we call that Plan B, yeah." Seb sat with Hallie on a nearby table to keep eye on the target without giving away their position.

"Give me 5 minutes." Hallie looked to Seb and he knew straight away he was not going to like this plan.

"Absolutely not."

"5 minutes, I can get him out and heading up to his room and you can meet us there, sure Wren would be happy to assist you."

"With fucking pleasure, on my way. Boris take my position." Wren was already heading down to the van to grab a suit and ticket from Katie so he could get entry for this event.

"Hallie, he is probably one of the most dangerous men out there, I won't risk you."

"He isn't the most dangerous man out there. You are and you are mine, so I am safe. Everyone has eyes on me, Katie and Gibb you got camera footage of the elevators?"

"Sure do."

"5 minutes, if that doesn't work then I will leave and come back and can-do Plan B."

Seb looked around the room not happy with this plan, but it was the best they had. "5 minutes. I am timing this darl."

"Wouldn't expect any different."

"Can I just ask what this plan is as I am confused?" Gibb questioned as he was tuning in the radio system the police use to communicate.

"Watch and learn Gibb. See how much Hallie can act for this."

Hallie began to walk over to the VIP entrance however noticing it was ticket access only, she showed her ticket to the security man who allowed her entry. There was a seat either side of the target which was obviously there so no one could be too close to him. Hallie ignored this and went straight to one of the seats and asked the bar man for a Porn star Martini and a shot of tequila. This caught the attention of the target to which he looked Hallie up and down and approved of what he saw. By this time Wren was now in the building and sat with Seb ready to pounce if they needed too.

"Put that on my tab Tom would you".

"Oh really, you don't have to I am happy to pay."

"Nonsense, a woman like you should be spoiled. Who are you if you don't mind me asking?"

"My name is Anna Swift, and yours?" Hallie held out her hand to shake his awaiting his response.

"Charlie Henderson. What an intriguing name, are you from around here?" Charlie was a very well-built man, blonde hair with flakes of darkness through the roots. His eyes were a royal blue and had a clean shaved face. Wearing a black suit and tie anyone would think he was taking part in a men in black look alike competition as he had the black sunglasses on his head.

"No, was invited by a friend who has gone to have sex with one of the Lord's over there." This was a lie, but Hallie needed to get his attention somehow and what do men think most about, Sex.

"So, you're all alone now then".

"Looks that way." Hallie took her shot then began sipping her martini. "What about you, from around here?"

"I travel a lot. I own the penthouse here though so least I don't have far to go when I am done being sociable." Charlie began to chuckle; this unsettled Hallie's stomach however she needed to get him alone so he could be extracted.

"Penthouse, blimey must have some money, this building is huge the views must be amazing!"

"I can show you now if you like, bored here anyways, just old people. No one as interesting as you. Come on bring the drink if you like." Hallie got up and followed Charlie to the lift.

Seb stopped the timer and was showing that took her four minutes thirty-seven seconds. Wren looked over his shoulder to see the time. "That was impressive."

"If he touches her, I will kill him."

"You are going to kill him anyways mate." Wren looked over to Seb as they made their way to the penthouse following Hallie and Charlie.

"Okay, then I will break his fingers one by one before I kill him if he touches her. Better."

"Much better." Wren went along with the joke, but he knew Seb was being serious.

Gibb and Katie had footages of all the cameras in the building and watched as Hallie and Charlie went up in the lift. "Well, he hasn't touched her yet sir, that is a good sign. Oh wait, nope he has her waist." Gibb thought he was helping however made Seb angrier causing him to clench his fists as the lift was going up.

"Yeah Gibb, not helping on that one. Where are they now."

"They have just entered the Penthouse and, the door is now closed we don't have eyes anymore."

"Okay, Boris, do you have eyes through the window?"

"Yes sir, all okay so far, he has just led down on the bed whilst Hallie is looking round the suite."

"Perfect, she is stalling. We are outside wait for our call okay."

"Yes sir."

"Perfect, you ready Seb."

"Never been more ready."

Three sharp knocks at the door make Charlie confused, "Oh, I told the bar to send up champagne, I paid for it as a thank you for the drinks and getting me out that event." This caused Charlie to lay back down on the bed and relax.

"Well, aren't you something else, how has no one claimed you yet." As Charlie had said this Hallie had already opened the door to Seb and Wren.

"Someone already has." With that a Seb pulled out a gun and shot him in the shoulder. A clear wound making sure no arteries or bone was hit just a flesh wound which made Charlie fall to the floor. Wren and Seb pulled him back up and tied him to the chair by the window so Boris would have the perfect shot if he needed it.

"You lying little bitch." That comment didn't sit well with Seb either causing another hit to the face.

"I mean, you must be desperate, how long did it take me to get him out of there."

"Just over four minutes darl, pretty impressive."

"Why thank you."

"Do you know who the fuck I am!" Charlie was now shouting and pulling his arms trying to free himself.

"We do, do you know who the fuck we are?" Charlie looked at all three of them standing in front of him to which it finally clicked. He knew who they were and why they were here.

"Finally found me huh, you know they will find you before you are able to do anything to me."

"Nope, see that suitcase, you will be in it soon and knocked out so we can take you to another location where you will stay until we get all the answers. Unless you are willing to communicate now?"

"Go fuck yourselves".

All three of them looked at each other and smiled. Hallie reached into Seb's pocket and then kissed his neck before walking behind Charlie. "Have it your way then." From this she stabbed the long needle into his neck, injecting a drug straight into his system causing his vision to start going blurry. To which when he woke up, he was in Seb's basement, tied up in the same chains used on Fowler.

"Hello, anyone. Get me the fuck out of here. You are all dead you hear. Dead!"

"Best you start talking Charlie boy, already killed three of your men for being fucking idiots. You will die and I will take great pleasure in making sure it is slow and painful." Seb was sat in the same chair in the corner, he knew Charlie would crack eventually and would enjoy every minute of him being chained like an animal.

"Fine, what do you want from me huh?"

"The truth, names, the person behind it all. Start talking Charlie, got plenty of time on my hands and plenty of body parts I can break, rip off and tear until you die."

"My boss is Harold Kingston."

"You're lying." Seb stood up in shock from this name, he didn't believe it at all.

"I swear I swear. He took me on five years ago, he gave me everything. I ran the show with his instructions so it would never trace back to him."

"Who else knows about him?"

"My brother, Jake. He is his personal human shield. We work together. Please man, let me go."

"You know, your name has been on my radar for some time. Now I have you, you are not getting away that easy." Seb walked away turning the lights off and headed up the stairs locking the door behind him. He went into the lounge where everyone was already eating except Hallie who waited for Seb like she does every night. Seb kissed Hallie before sitting down and grabbing his food.

"We have a name."

"Already? What did you do to him?"

"Hadn't even touched him yet. But we need to run checks behind this because if it is who he says it is, this just took a turn for the worse."

"Who?"

"Harold Kingston. Charlie's brother knows about it all so we need to find him, get the same name from him and get him to admit all of the fucked up shit they have done and then can go in that way."

"Fuck off." Wren was gob smacked by this response as were the rest of them.

"Hallie? You good"

"Yeah, sorry just need a drink, I'll be right back." Seb knew something wasn't right so placing his food on the coffee table he followed Hallie to the kitchen.

"Darl, you know him. Don't you."

"Yes."

"How?"

"He was my foster parent, the last one, the one that encouraged me to go into the army, make a name for myself. That was the family that I thought truly cared but really wanted me gone at 16." Hallie began sipping her water when Seb came up behind her and turned her around.

"He now is one of our targets, are you okay with that?"

"Yes, I am fine. Just shocked me at first. I'm fine let's go back in." Hallie began to walk away before Seb pulled her back and looked her straight in the eyes.

"You're a bad liar, but I am here when you are ready. Okay."

"Thank you."

Multiple footsteps which sounded like running came straight for the kitchen which interrupted Hallie and Seb's moment. Both looking up to see everyone in a panic.

"What?"

"We need to go now; they have just put a new target out."

"But Charlie is here, how is that possible."

"The big boss must be taking control in his absence."
"Where is it?"
"Winchester Constabulary, we need to go there now."

Acknowledgements

Firstly, I would like to thank everyone for your kind words and support throughout me writing this book. I have received so much positivity which has encouraged me to write. This book has been the setting stone to a dream career I have forever wanted to achieve.

I would like to thank my amazing partner who has been there for me through thick and thin, letting me read parts of the book I didn't know if I liked and being my rock.

My family who has been so proud and inspired me to pursue this dream.
Never knowing how this book will turn out I will forever be grateful to share my hobby with the world hoping they love escaping just as much as I do.

Thank you to my closest friends- (you know who you are) for sharing the excitement I had when I shared I was writing this book.

Having a love for reading from such a young age really has helped me in this writing process. So many inspiring authors who have helped me escape reality and into their imagination with the turn of a page.

Thank you to those who have tried the book and loved the journey and are keen for the next one and to those who didn't like the book thank you for reading it still and giving me a chance.

I look forward to seeing how this pans out but in the meantime all I have to say is thank you.

Love Paige x

Printed in Great Britain
by Amazon